WOMEN IN

By Natalie

WOMEN IN CHARGE

Contents

DEDICATION

Women In Charge is dedicated with love and affection to all authoritative girls everywhere who are dating and still looking for that special guy. We all have lessons to learn before our prince comes our way.

PREFACE. Women In Charge

I have had many suitors along my path to finding my true love. More than a few of them had less than honorable intentions.

I learned quite a bit about boys in my early years. A woman named Vivian Becker taught me much about humiliating submissive types. I once knew a boy named Dean Livingstone and he was my secret lover. There were also others who tried to win my hand. Among them Timothy Elsmore and Clint Steele also tried their very best.

You might say that Mr. Right has yet to come my way. Finding a submissive male to do my bidding is not all that easy. Though I have teased many and had fun with them all there are days when I feel that I am doomed to a lifetime of domestic drudgery.

I hope that you enjoy the story.

CHAPTER 1. Mattie's Custom Lingerie

Mom wanted me to work that summer so she talked with a friend of hers about getting me a job. Jobs weren't easy to get so when Mom arranged for me to work for Mattie Gibson at *Mattie's Custom Lingerie* I was thrilled.

The shop was located on Main Street conveniently nestled between the *All About You* dress shop and the *A Girl Can Never Have Too Many* shoe shop. Back then Main Street was a dream. Also on the street was *the All Junior Girls* dress shop, the *Pretty Girl* spa and salon, the *Fancy Me* jewelry store and of course *Sally's Career Apparel* uniform shop.

The names alone take me down memory lane. My first dress came from *All Junior Girls* and my first earrings came from *Fancy Me*. They were clip-ons because Mom refused to let me get my ears pierced at such a young age. I could never forget my first perm and my first pedicure were with Mom at *Pretty Girl*.

Less memorable were my visits to *Sally's*. Every year before I went off to school in those dreaded uniforms I had to go there for new clothes. While we had our own mini garment district right in town fashion never really visited *Sally's* even though I had to.

The uniform shop sold drab all-weather school uniforms, modern nurse apparel and waitress uniforms. They also carried a small selection of housekeeping uniforms for the local hotels.

While time has taken a toll on this kind of retail a few shops still remain. The stores were definitely reminders of an earlier time before shopping malls, warehouse stores and Internet shopping. Regardless of the heavy competition there was still clientele who came to *Mattie's Custom Lingerie* for the experience of personalized service and of course custom fit.

Parking was well down the street in a public lot. So during the day women would stroll past *Mattie's* on their way to the other stores. So there was always a steady stream of foot traffic that assured the success of the lingerie shop.

I remember as a young girl being embarrassed by the mannequins in the shop window. A girl passing by could see lady's unmentionables in full view. Past the pretty lingerie clad models you could see the ladies shopping inside. I had thought that boys shouldn't be privy to seeing such things.

Mattie was an older woman who boasted that when it came to lingerie she had seen it all. Mattie had never married so her shop was her life. She had the appearance of a rather stern school teacher while at the same time she was a lovely lady who could pleasantly talk with customers.

Of course I was so young that I had no idea what working in a custom lingerie shop entailed. I didn't even know why a woman would want to have custom lingerie. I quickly learned that most women are wearing the wrong size bra. Poorly fitted bras are uncomfortable and don't provide anywhere near the necessary support. Poorly fitted shaping garments have similar issues.

We didn't actually manufacture anything on the premises. Aside from the inventory that was on hand — you know Bali, Playtex, Maidenform, Spanx and all the rest of the usual stuff — all of the special work was outsourced to several custom workshops.

So a big part of the job was to measure women for a proper fit and before taking their order. The store had two fitting rooms at the back that were separated by a platform no longer in use that I presumed had previously been reserved for a mannequin display. The display would have been visible from the street down the aisle that divided the store into ladies bras and panties on one side and classic heavy full foundation garments on the other.

I learned that there was more to ladies foundation garments than just function. While most of us don't think much of our lingerie other than mere function I discovered that there are women who use lingerie for sexual purposes. Not only can lingerie give a lady the curves she desires it also can have a desirable fetish effect on certain guys.

Mattie never advertised her shop. Women found us by referral from friends. We had many longtime customers who came in regularly for purchases and we also had young girls who came in for their first real fittings.

The Wonderbra was a favorite of the young girls. Once I discovered the benefits I too wore them while I worked at the shop and for special dates. I always felt more mature and more attractive with the support that I received from the garments. Most young girls select an improper Wonderbra but at *Mattie's Custom Lingerie* we sent them down the right path.

4

Our older clientele accounted for great repeat business. These women often brought daughters with them to the shop so that was how we got new customers. These ladies shopped with us because they liked the attention and the fit that good service provided. They also liked to have their daughters fitted for classic full length overbust corsets. Not because they needed the curves but because they were virtually impossible to penetrate. A girl couldn't get any pleasure wearing one so they were perfect for young teens dating for the first time.

Mattie taught me how to take a customer back into the fitting rooms and properly measure her. Mattie preferred the old-fashioned method — having the customer disrobe before measuring — but I found that younger girls were more comfortable being measured over their existing lingerie.

Despite the possible illusion of glamour that a job like that might present the work was really quite mundane. At least it was until the day that Mrs. Becker came into the shop.

CHAPTER 2. Mrs. Becker

Mattie saw Mrs. Becker walking up to the shop through the big front window. She immediately whispered instructions to me. She told me that Mrs. Vivian Becker was an important customer and that I was only to observe how she took care of a prized customer and not to say a word until she left the shop.

The door opened and Mrs. Becker along with her domestic maid made their entrance. I remember how impressed I was with Mrs. Becker. The sight of a woman shopping with her maid was quite unusual. These days a full-time domestic maid is simply unheard of. The practice harkened back to the nineteenth century when such luxury was more affordable.

In fact Mrs. Becker was the first woman who I ever observed shopping with her maid. I thought that she must be of significant means to be able to employ such an indulging pleasure. No wonder Mattie thought of her to be such an important customer.

How did I know that the girl was her maid? It was unmistakable. The girl couldn't be anything other than her maid. She walked a few steps behind Mrs. Becker like a proper domestic. She wore the common black and white trimmed uniform that likely came from *Sally's* that screamed servant. If that wasn't enough her matching apron and mob cap were both a dead giveaway. Of course the fancy embroidery on her uniform that said *Maid Daisy* helped too.

Apparently it wasn't enough for Mrs. Becker to put the girl's name on her uniform she had to state her rank too. I knew that *Sally's* did embroidery because I had seen it before on waitresses in town but those girls typically only had their name on their uniform.

I suppose given her clear upper class status it was appropriate for Mrs. Becker to state the obvious on her servant for all to see. I would most likely do the same given the identical circumstances. Why wouldn't I also do the same? After all the origin of the servant's uniform was to draw a well-defined line between employer and her staff. Mrs. Becker was simply going along with tradition.

While Mrs. Becker's hands were free Maid Daisy was carrying packages from *All About You, A Girl Can Never Have Too Many* and *Sally's*. She was also holding a purse that I presumed belonged to Mrs. Becker. I wondered what it must be like to be shopping like that with someone right there to hold your packages. I only dreamed for a moment because I knew that I would most likely never be able to afford that sort of pampering.

Mrs. Becker went straight up to Mattie and began chatting with her. I stayed back behind the register simply observing the discussion between the two ladies. Maid Daisy stayed back simply content to hold her purse and packages.

Finally after pleasantries were exchanged Mrs. Becker got to the purpose of her visit. I overheard her mention that the full length girdle that she had previously purchased for Daisy was fine but that she wanted something more secure for her.

Daisy followed closely behind Mrs. Becker while Mattie led the way towards the fitting rooms. When Mattie passed by the register she motioned for me to follow and to bring pen and paper to take down measurements.

Oddly, and to my surprise, Mattie stopped at the pedestal between the dressing rooms and motioned for Daisy to step up. I have to say that I was shocked when Mattie ordered the woman to take her dress off so that she could be measured.

While Mattie went into the back room for a moment Mrs. Becker calmly watched while Daisy remove her apron, unbutton her dress and placed them both on a hook that was on the wall behind her. I felt embarrassed for Daisy. She stood there on the platform in one of our custom classic full length overbust corsets with her stockings attached with garter tabs in full view of any passer-by who might take a glance into the shop. It was quite unusual to say the least.

Things became stranger when Mattie emerged from the back room wearing pink disposable gloves — the kind you might wear when washing dishes — only these were a bit finer fit that was suitable for more detailed work.

While I was fascinated with what happened next Mrs. Becker seemed rather nonchalant about the scene that unfolded. Mattie casually undid the garter tabs and Daisy's stockings sagged on her thighs. Then she told the girl to spread her legs. Then Mattie unhooked the crotch before carefully rolling the girdle up to Daisy's waist.

I couldn't believe my eyes. With her corset up exposing her genitals Daisy was clearly not a woman though up to that point there had been an obvious lack of male features on the maid. I

9

wanted to divert my eyes from the—and nice girls don't like to use this word but there is no other way—*penis* that was in full view but I couldn't. No matter how hard I tried my eyes stayed riveted to the bizarre scene.

For me it was a first. It was one thing to measure a naked woman in the soft shadows and privacy of a dressing room but it was an entirely different experience to see a *penis* out in the shop open to casual inspection.

Of course my youthful eyes took full advantage of the rare opportunity to see a male sex organ in the full light of day. I wondered how such a flaccid little thing could possibly be the center of male ego. Then I reminded myself that a *penis*— oh I said it again!—could impregnate a woman and cause her months of uncomfortable grief.

Mattie proceeded like seeing a male in such a condition was commonplace. She casually took her garment tape out of her dress pocket and looked up at Daisy.

"I'm going to measure you for your chastity. I will warn you in advance just like the last time you were here that this is not meant to be pleasurable. There will be consequences for an erection or even if I detect even a dribble of excitement. Do you understand me?"

She said it with such authority that even I was frightened by her tone. Daisy meekly responded with "Yes Madam Mattie" before Mattie proceeded to take her measurements.

I was not sure if all of the measurements that were taken were necessary or if Mattie was just enjoying humiliating the blushing Daisy. For whatever reason Mattie called out, and I recorded, everything from the circumference of the penis from the tip to behind the scrotum along with the length of everything in between.

She certainly took her time about it. She turned the penis this way and that way. At one point she gave it a tug and measured the length. She tugged on the little scrotum and gave the testicles a squeeze before taking a measurement.

Through all of the pulling, squeezing and measuring the penis remained obediently flaccid and not a dribble of precum appeared. I have no idea what the penalty may have been for such forbidden behavior but I was glad for Daisy that I didn't have to find out.

Honestly I've personally had pelvic exams that took less time and were certainly less intrusive than what Mattie did with Daisy. I certainly enjoyed watching the exhibition. I found myself engrossed in the detail. A girl always finds the male sex organ to be an object of idle curiosity and I'm certainly no different than any other woman in that regard.

I'm not ashamed to also say that I found it all to be erotic in a naughty sort of way. My heart pounded away while I took notes and I felt moist in a place where good girls shouldn't. I didn't feel guilty. All of it was seemingly justified because it was Mattie who was taking measurements for what I was sure was a noble purpose. It was my job to pay close attention and record every captivating detail.

It seemed like forever before she finally declared that she had everything that she needed to ensure a good snug fit. Just at that moment a couple of ladies came into the shop and began to browse. When they noticed Daisy they giggled and whispered to each other but they then continued to shop.

Mattie told me to see to the customers. While I listened to them tell me what they were looking for — something about a bra for a full figured woman— I saw Daisy clip her stockings back up and then put her dress back on.

Mattie led Mrs. Becker and Daisy back to the register where she wrote up their order. I overheard her mention that custom chastity devices take a couple of weeks to come in and that she would call when the order was received.

When she said the words custom chastity device my customers giggled again. They burst out in hysterical laughter when Mrs. Becker finally led Daisy back out of the shop.

I quickly finished up with my customers because I could hardly wait to ask Mattie questions about Mrs. Becker.

CHAPTER 3. *Mattie Explains All*

"Natalie I'm sure that you have questions."

What an understatement! I hardly knew where to begin. Mattie spared me the trouble. She immediately began to talk about Mrs. Becker.

"Daisy married well. Vivian runs the family business and when Dillon — that was her husband's name back then — married her she gave him a management job at her company.

Everything was fine until Vivian found Dillon doing — shall we say — serious in depth business with his secretary. The young tart was a beauty named Daisy. Vivian arrived just in time to spoil their orgasms and cheat them out of their bawdy pleasure. Naturally Vivian was outraged at such a disgraceful scene. She chased the half-naked secretary right out of the building and tossed her clothes out the front door into the street.

Of course she could never trust him again after that so she intended on divorcing him. Thankfully she had a good prenuptial so he would have been left with nothing.

He begged her to stay on so she relented but only under certain conditions. Since Dillon admired Daisy so much Vivian thought that Dillon should emulate his secretary. So the condition was that Dillon was to become Daisy her secretary at the office and her maid in her home. Daisy would wear female clothing and would live and act just like a woman. At the office Daisy wears her hair just like her secretary did and even wears similar outfits. It was only under those terms that Dillon, I mean Daisy, was allowed to stay."

I stopped Mattie at that point and asked a question.

"But why did she want him to look like a woman?"

"That's a good question Natalie. The answer is that Vivian wanted to make sure that Daisy never cheated on her again. That was also why she was here today — to have Daisy measured for a chastity device. The sissy girl is still ill-disciplined so Vivian didn't want to take any chances."

"I didn't know we did that here."

"It's part of our intimate service offerings, along with silicone breast forms and a wide assortment of dildos and strapon harnesses."

"I noticed Daisy's breasts. I thought they were real."

"No, I sold them to her a few weeks back."

I took a moment to consider everything that I had seen.

"But Mattie why such a public display of humiliation? Couldn't Mrs. Becker have just privately used Daisy inside of her home?"

Mattie shook her head.

"Public humiliation of the male is the ultimate expression of female superiority. What better way to show off her authority than to parade her husband around like a common housemaid? You have to admit it is quite a display of feminine power. It also serves like a warning to other males that Vivian is a force to be reckoned with and will not yield to male bravado."

I thought that I understood. I had another question. I was a bit embarrassed but I had to know.

"If Daisy is in chastity won't Mrs. Becker be giving up sex?"

Mattie laughed.

"No not at all. Vivian enjoys oral servitude. Sissy girls — and that's what Daisy is now — can be trained to be quite adept at it. Soon she'll have her chastity belt and when she is attired in female clothing the sissy won't have any other choice.

Instead of wasting time on her own pleasure Daisy will learn just like other sissy girls that the pleasure of her Mistress is more important than her own. She will feel a certain suspenseful euphoria serving her Mistress that is actually quite addictive. It won't be too long before she won't remember a time when she didn't long to serve."

"Did you say other sissy girls?"

"Oh yes, many others. Daisy was not the first to shamefully display her submission to women on the pedestal and she certainly won't be the last. Many sissy girls have worn the belt of shame. Our long time customers have seen it before. Many straying husbands have been put on display attired in a similar manner.

Plus should any woman happen to get as far as that chastity device they will immediately see that Daisy is spoken for and under complete feminine control. So between her attire and her chastity device Vivian can be certain that Daisy won't be straying anytime soon."

The idea of a male under the complete control of a woman made my face flush with arousal. The possibilities of male submission bending to my will complete with oral sex on demand was new and exciting. Mattie seemed to read my mind.

"I can see that I've given you something new to think about. Exhilarating isn't it? Some might say liberating. After all you've seen today I'm sure that you'll have trouble sleeping tonight. I've got something special that might help you out."

She went behind the counter and brought out a brand new phallic shaped vibrator that was still in the package. She gave it to me.

"Trust me you'll sleep much better tonight."

I did. It was the best use of AA batteries ever!

CHAPTER 4. Chastity

When Mrs. Becker's order came in a few weeks later Mattie gave me the same instructions to stay silent and simply observe. Again Daisy was marched to the platform and she was ordered to take off her dress.

While I held the chastity belt Mattie unhooked Daisy's girdle and rolled it up to her waist. She used baby powder on the penis before she carefully fitted the metal cage over it and secured it in place with a metal ring behind the scrotum and with a tiny lock. The whole ensemble was completed with a leather belt that Mattie locked in place with another little lock. The key to the locks was on a chain which she then presented Mrs. Becker. Mrs. Becker placed it around her neck and the key dangled in full view between her breasts.

Daisy stood there looking quite timid in her new accessory. I could tell by the tight fit that Daisy would not be having any unsanctioned erections any time soon. Her little penis was completely confined and totally unable to offer any pleasure to any woman without the full consent of Mrs. Becker.

Mattie had Daisy remain standing with her chastity belt showing while she rang up the purchase for Mrs. Becker. I found the obvious power of the women over Daisy to be extremely erotic. My mind quickly went to the vibrator that Mattie had provided me with and I couldn't wait to get back home to put it to good use.

Mrs. Becker casually spoke with Mattie while Daisy stood at attention. Several female customers came into the shop. While one of them never noticed the display of male submission two of the others actually walked up to Daisy and laughed at her predicament.

It was only after those customers left and Mattie finished a long discussion with Mrs. Becker that Daisy was permitted to dress. When they left the shop it would be the last time I would ever see Mrs. Becker or Daisy.

That night the image of Daisy standing in her chastity belt stayed vividly in my head while my magic vibrator did its heavenly work. At the same time I wondered how Mrs. Becker felt when Daisy pleasured her with her tongue. I decided that I needed to know much more about male submission to women and sissy girl behavior. My earth shaking orgasm reinforced my own desire to experience the domination of a male one day for myself.

I graduated from college before the next summer so I left the employ of *Mattie's Custom Lingerie*. But it was the image of Daisy in her maid uniform that changed my impression of boys forever.

Before Daisy I saw the world of boys in simple terms. I had always thought of boys to be like a single flavor of ice cream. I thought vanilla boys to be stronger and smarter than girls. I thought a girl's lot in life was to serve and pleasure the boy who deemed her worthy enough to marry.

Of course that was nonsense. Daisy taught me that like ice cream there was also strawberry, black cherry and an assortment of others to choose from. My job was to find the boy equivalent of chocolate — my very favorite flavor.

I learned that not all boys were rogues who were only interested in getting into a girl's undies. Others wanted to serve women and could be trained to do just about anything we desired — including carrying our purse and packages when we shopped. Not to mention doing all of the household chores.

I had no idea how to find such a boy. But at least I knew that they existed.

After *Mattie's Custom Lingerie* I found an office job with a big company where I went to work in the same department with my best friend Carol Richardson.

It was there that I met Timothy Elsmore. We dated for months and things became quite intense. All the while I dated Timothy I still couldn't get the vision of Daisy standing in her chastity belt out of my mind. There was something about the sexual power of women over males that I found absolutely intriguing.

I wasn't sure if Timothy was my special guy. But still things progressed quickly with Timothy.

CHAPTER 5. A Proposal

I held the ring out in the palm of my hand so that Mom could see it. It was a silver setting with tiny little diamonds surrounding a rather substantial stone. It was elegant, tasteful and certainly very expensive. It was truly representative of Timothy's love for me. All I had to do was say yes and I would be Mrs. Timothy Elsmore.

It was my very first proposal and I felt like I had been swept off my feet into a heavenly place reserved only for the luckiest of women. Mother wasn't so impressed.

"Did you say that he proposed like a proper gentleman?"

"Absolutely. It was quite a scene. We had dinner, there was candlelight and violins were playing. He went down on one knee and he asked me if I would be his bride and live with him forever."

"Natalie you're really too young to be married. What did you tell him?"

"That's why I wanted to talk with you. After he proposed I took the ring and everyone in the restaurant applauded. But he interrupted me before I could answer him."

"How rude and thoughtless of him. So why on earth did he do that to you dear?"

"He said that he had to tell me something before I answered him."

She rolled her eyes.

"Oh? Pray tell what did poor lovesick Timothy have to say for himself?"

Mother had always seemed to like Timothy. He came around quite frequently and she often said he was cute and very polite. I think the word she had used most often was adorable. I had always suspected that perhaps Mom thought a bit *too* highly of him so her lukewarm response to his proposal was a little bit of a surprise. I hated to burst her bubble but I had to explain further.

"He said before I answered that I needed to know something about him. I have to admit that he took me totally by surprise. He told me that he likes to occasionally crossdress."

At first it didn't seem to register with Mom. She paused for a wistful moment before she casually commented.

"Crossdress?"

"Right, crossdress. You know, he likes to wear women's clothing."

"I know what that means Natalie. I just never imagined Timothy being like that. I can see a cute and adorable Timothy — yes. But sissy girl Timothy? My goodness who would ever think such a thing? So why aren't you wearing the ring?"

I put the ring on my finger. I showed her that it was at least a size or two too big for my finger. Then I put the ring back into my purse so that I wouldn't lose it.

"I didn't answer him. I wanted to talk to you first."

"I see. What do you expect *me* to do about panty boy?"

"Mom it's not like that. You know Timothy he's straight as an arrow. But I do want your advice. What should I do?"

Again Mom paused to consider her answer. After a few moments of reflective contemplation she gave me a smile.

"You have to understand things about boys who crossdress. There are of course many *possibilities* with such a situation but strong virile companionship is not very likely."

She had stressed the word *possibilities* in an odd manner. I had no idea what she meant by that.

"More likely you'll find that you have a sensitive caring husband who is most interested in feminine things. You know, cooking, cleaning and laundry. He probably likes to knit too. Crossdressers are not strong masculine men. They tend to be submissive sorts who like to be dominated by women. Is that the kind of guy you are looking for?"

I couldn't disagree fast enough.

"Timothy's not like that. No, he's not submissive to women."

"Are you sure? You may be getting into a lifetime of having to see to his feminine needs. Next thing you know you'll be buying him falsies for his brassiere and putting him to bed in curlers."

"Really Mom? Don't overstate this."

"A girl should have a strong virile man between her legs when she has the need for pleasure. Do you think that a sissy boy like Timothy can provide you with that?"

"Mother!"

"I'll tell you what. Bring him around tomorrow and I'll talk with you both. Then I'll tell you what I think."

It sounded like a good idea at the time.

CHAPTER 6. The Interview

It was Sunday afternoon—a perfect time for Timothy to visit with us. Mom was sitting in her home office behind her mahogany desk appearing quite authoritative. I had often sat in one of the two chairs that were in front of the desk while she advised me on matters of importance. She always seemed so imposing behind her big desk. Perhaps that was her plan. I answered the front door and brought Timothy into her office. We both sat down and waited for Mom to begin.

She took her time. She finished with some paperwork while we patiently watched her work. With a final shuffle she pushed the papers aside and looked straight at Timothy.

"So Timothy you want to marry my Natalie?

"That's right Alicia. She is the love of my life."

Timothy always called Mom by her first name. For some reason it seemed too casual under the circumstances. Mom gave him a long stare.

"You seem too young to marry. I think that perhaps you are more boy than man. A married man needs substantial wherewithal to see to the demanding needs of a real woman. How do you plan on providing for my daughter?"

In spite of Moms rude insinuation he smiled that charming boyish smile that he so often flashes.

"I work at the local paper. I hope to put my degree to good use and become a reporter one day."

"What are you doing there?"

"I'm in distribution."

"Oh, I see. You're a paper boy.

He cringed at how she had belittled his position at the paper. I knew that he was actually in charge of the Internet site where the news was posted but the company stilled used an old department name and called that distribution.

"I suppose that it could be worse. At least you have a job. I suppose that you expect a traditional marriage? Do you anticipate having Natalie doing all of the housework? Do you envision my Natalie cooking, cleaning and doing your laundry?"

He glanced at me and grinned.

"Yes, of course I do. She'll make a great housewife."

We hadn't talked about division of household chores. Was that what he was thinking? I sure couldn't think of anything more repulsive than that revolting thought. Domestic work isn't exactly my thing. I hadn't given much thought to how our housekeeping would be done once I was married.

Mom was not impressed either. Housekeeping really isn't her thing either. With a negative nod and bit of a frown Mother continued on.

"I see. Well let me get to the point. Natalie has told me that you are a sissy boy and that you enjoy wearing women's clothing. Is that true?"

I thought that Timothy was going to fall out of his chair and pass out. I guess I should have warned him that I had told Mom everything that he had said. Why wouldn't I? His face flushed a deep red while he attempted to gather himself. Mom didn't wait for him to answer. Instead she continued on.

"That's not very manly of you now is it? Be truthful with me. You do enjoy wearing women's clothing don't you? There is quite an allure to soft fabrics isn't there? Tell me, are you wearing feminine panties right now?"

Timothy was certainly flustered. He tried to form a word but Mom wouldn't let him talk.

"What about your legs? Do you shave them like a girl?"

"Mother stop!"

She smiled at me.

"I've seen enough dear. You may both go. I'll speak with you later."

Timothy quickly stood up and we left Mom's office together. Once we were safely outside we paused to gather ourselves out on the porch.

"You could have warned me."

"I'm so sorry. I never thought that she would do anything like that."

We kissed goodbye and I went back inside the house.

31

"Mother how could you?"

"I was testing him. Did you see how docile he was?"

"You surprised him."

"Did I? A more virile man would have done better. I'm surprised that he didn't attempt to duck under your skirt for cover. Of course I would never have to pose those kinds of questions to a masculine hunk of a man."

"Oh please Mom…"

"You'll be sorry if you marry him. Tell him no."

"But I like him."

"Like is not love. Fireworks should go off and he should take your breath away with his strong virile body. A girl needs what a girl needs and dear I just don't see it in Timothy."

"I don't believe you."

"I'll tell you what. Bring him by again next Saturday morning and I'll prove it to you."

"Promise to be nice."

"I promise. I'll be *very* nice."

I didn't like the way she said that.

CHAPTER 7. Cleaning Day

Saturday was always cleaning day at Mom's house. For years it had been my brother Stevie's duty to do all of the chores. But Stevie was away at college so Mom and I would work together every Saturday getting the house in perfect shape. Usually Mom wore an old housedress while she worked and I wore an old tank top and jeans. But this Saturday was different.

When the doorbell rang Mom went to answer it. She was wearing a little black party dress. It was a short little number that she wore when going out for the evening. The dress was extremely flattering on her and gave her the appearance of a college coed. In that dress there wasn't much left to the imagination.

If I dressed up similarly I'm certain that we could have both gone out and nobody would suspect that we were Mother and daughter. I didn't get the message though so I was just in my usual jeans and tank top. Her attire was my first clue that Mom had something special planned for my suitor.

I peeked out of the office to see Timothy's response to my Mother's attire. His eyes nearly popped out of his head while he followed her back into her office where I was waiting. I suppose that was to be expected because I look very much like Mom. Nevertheless his wandering eye was disturbing. I made a mental note to talk to him about that later.

Thankfully Mom sat down behind her desk so at least her legs were modestly concealed from his gaze. Timothy sat down next to me.

"Timothy I've considered your affinity for women's clothing."

"Alicia it's not really what I would call an affinity…"

"Oh really? We'll see about that."

There was an uncomfortable silence before Mom continued. Now she was looking at me while ignoring Timothy.

"There are ways to handle sissy boys like Timothy with their little addiction. They need to be shown their place. I understand that you don't believe what I've told you about sissy boys so I've arranged a little demonstration for you."

She turned her attention back to Timothy.

"You are to go upstairs to the guest bedroom that is on the left side of the hallway. There you will find suitable attire for today waiting for you on the bed. Change your clothes and report back here immediately."

Timothy looked at me. I shrugged my shoulders. Mom continued.

"If you want to marry my daughter you won't waste any more of my time. You'll do precisely like you are told to do. Otherwise you may leave us but then we don't ever want to see you again."

Timothy didn't need any more encouragement than that. He immediately stood up and went up the stairs.

"Mom, what's going on?"

"You'll see dear. I just want you to see the real Timothy for yourself."

It seemingly took forever before Timothy returned. When I finally heard him coming down the stairs I was relieved that he didn't keep us waiting any longer.

CHAPTER 8. Meek Entrance

I heard steps walking near to Mom's office but for some reason Timothy didn't enter. From where I was sitting I couldn't see him but Mom obviously could.

"Don't be shy dear. Come in so that we can both have a good look at you."

There was a pause before he stepped into the room. I couldn't believe my eyes. There was Timothy, or at least a person who I thought was Timothy, dressed in a black maid uniform complete with matching apron and lace cap!

I can't overstate the transformation that had taken place. The uniform was similar to what is typical for a common hotel maid. It was black with white trim and it had *Maid Tillie* embroidered on it. He was wearing mid-height black patent heels. I couldn't help but notice — his legs *were* shaved. Not only that but Timothy was wearing a feminine brunet wig under the maid cap with curly locks that flowed to his shoulders. The final touch was that he had applied makeup to his face — a hint of blush, lipstick and even eyeshadow with mascara.

I have to admit that the remarkable transformation was quite impressive. Had I not been expecting Timothy to come through the door I would have thought that Mom had hired herself a real maid.

I was speechless as the maid self-consciously walked in. I was appalled at how easily Mom had turned my beau into such a demure looking domestic maid. He was just about to sit down when Mom intervened.

"I didn't say that you could sit dear. I believe that dressed the way that you are it is appropriate for you to stand at attention in our presence and wait for your instructions. Plus if you know what's best for you then you won't speak unless spoken to."

The maid stood just like she had been ordered to do. Mom looked straight at me.

"You see that the submissive male is easily controlled by an authoritative woman. A male who enjoys the feel of women's clothing will repeatedly dress himself like a woman until he can no longer resist the allure. The submissive sissy finds it all to be rather erotic. Clearly the presence of the maid uniform was far too much for this sissy girl to resist. There are of course benefits to be had which I will endeavor to show you today."

I was so shocked that I still couldn't think of a thing to say. Timothy didn't help out. He simply stood at attention just like Mom had ordered him to do like he was a household servant. She turned her gaze to him.

"Now sweetie today is cleaning day in this house and you will be doing all of the chores today. Dressed the way you are I can't think of a better use of your time."

"But Alicia…"

"Silence!

She yelled at the top of her voice. I hadn't heard her speak that loudly since my brother Stevie was a little boy and was in need of a well-deserved spanking.

"Did I say that you could speak? You must not speak unless spoken to. You had best understand that in this house I am the Mistress of the Manor and that you will be respectful to me at all times. Get it in your silly little head that I am in charge here. From now on I am Madam Deshay to you and this lovely daughter of mine is Miss Deshay."

When she said Miss Deshay she pointed to me
and then she looked back at him.

"We are both clearly your superiors and so you
will address us properly. Is that understood?"

Just like that he had been put in his place. The
maid lowered her gaze and responded with a soft
meek voice.

"Yes Madam Deshay."

"Since you enjoy female clothing so much it
would be a shame for you to wear anything else
when you enter my home. From now on I expect
you in uniform as soon as you arrive. You will
keep your uniforms in the guest room and you
will change there.

Such a pretty looking sissy girl can't possibly be
called Timothy can she? From now on you are
maid Tillie just like it says on your uniform. Do
you understand me girl? Well?"

He seemed confused for a moment before he
realized that she expected a response.

"Yes Madam Deshay."

"A quick learner. I like that in a maid."

Mom looked at me.

"Natalie do you still have that wedding ring?"

"Of course."

"May I see it?"

I took it out of my purse and gave it to Mom. She handed it to Tillie.

"Put this on your finger girl. We wouldn't want an eager suitor to spirit you away."

Tillie's hand was shaking when she slid the ring on. It fit her perfectly.

"It's time to put you to work Tillie. You will start today in the laundry room. I expect all of the clothes to be properly cleaned. That means hand washing lingerie. You are dismissed. Get to it."

Remarkably Tillie jumped right to it. I heard her heels clicking on the hallway tile while she scurried straight to the laundry room. Mom gave me a satisfied grin.

"Do you see the possibilities?"

"Of course I do. But did you have to humiliate him like that? The uniform was one thing but a wig and makeup? Isn't that overdoing it?"

Her eyes sparkled as she smiled.

"Natalie dear I told maid Tillie to change into the attire that was on the bed. I didn't say anything about the wig and the makeup that was on the vanity. She did that on her own. That was all Tillie dear. I suppose that she just couldn't resist herself. Quite womanly wouldn't you say?

I have always wanted a maid of my own dear. Always remember that boys come and they go, but a maid! Every woman needs a maid and once you have one you'll never want to go without!"

I rolled my eyes.

"Mom where did you get the uniform?"

"Just a little something special that I ordered just for the occasion. They wear the same outfit down at the Marriott. I think that proper couture is a necessity for every domestic maid—don't you think?"

I have to say that I couldn't think of a reason why not.

"She's perfect Mom. The *Maid Tillie* embroidery is a nice touch."

"Thank you dear. I thought it very appropriate given the circumstances. You had best go to the laundry room and supervise the maid. I fear that she doesn't know how to properly hand wash our lingerie."

CHAPTER 9. Tillie The Maid

Mom was right about Tillie. She definitely needed supervision in the laundry room. I had to show her how to fill the laundry sink and how to clean and pat dry our delicates. Then I had to show her how to sort clothes before loading the machine with the rest of our laundry.

Tillie didn't seem to mind the domestic work. She handled our lingerie with reverence and she smiled while she did her chores. For Tillie housekeeping appeared to be a labor of love. That was fine with me because I certainly didn't want any part of the domestic drudgery.

It was definitely not our usual Saturday. Mom and I lounged while Tillie did the work that the two of us would normally do. She not only did our laundry she dusted, vacuumed, did dishes and finally hand washed the tile floors. I sat with Mom in total disbelief of what was going on while Tillie was down on her hands and knees doing the floors.

"Natalie I hope that I've been able to show you a different side of Tillie. She does make a sweet maid doesn't she? But unless you have Sapphic tendencies I'm not so sure that she's marriage material."

I didn't say a word. But I already knew in the back of my mind that things would never be the same between us again. Mom was right. Tillie *was* quite feminine. But even if she would never share my bed maybe I did have other uses for her. Mom was thinking the same thing.

"Now that you've seen the real Tillie what do you think that we should do with her? I mean she is *extremely* submissive. She put that uniform on without even a complaint. What do you say we put her through her paces again next weekend?"

The thought of not having to do housework the following weekend was too much even for me to pass up.

"The sight of a male doing domestic housework was rather refreshing. Okay, why not?"

So when Tillie finally finished with the floors Mom told her that she was to report again the following Saturday. The maid meekly replied "Yes Madam Deshay" before Mom dismissed her like she would a common domestic maid.

CHAPTER 10. Second Saturday

Timothy arrived for work the following Saturday just like Mom had ordered. He went straight upstairs without saying a word and after a long delay Tillie emerged in uniform ready to get started with her chores. I was waiting in Mom's office while she fussed over paperwork when Tillie reported for duty.

Mom didn't even look up.

"Tillie there's laundry to do and the kitchen is a mess. Start in my private bathroom. See to it girl."

"Yes Madam Deshay."

Just like that Tillie was off. Only then did Mom look up from her work.

"Tillie is such a sweetheart darling isn't she? What do you think of your beau now?"

She giggled after that.

"Mom you're not being fair. Tillie...I mean Timothy...would make a good husband..."

She laughed.

"But a much better maid!"

Just then Tillie came back into the office.

"Please pardon me Madam Deshay. I need to restock the intimate feminine products in your bathroom. Do you keep extras?"

"In the hall closet dear."

"Thank you Madam."

Tillie was off again. Mom smiled at me.

"See what I mean? A few more weeks and I'll have Tillie sitting to pee like a good little girl. She simply can't resist herself. A maid uniform will do that to a sissy girl.

A sissy like that certainly won't be able to satisfy you the way a real man could. I doubt that she would be of much use for you in the bedroom other than with her tongue."

I was beginning to think that she was right. Just then there was a knock at the front door.

"Natalie would you please get that. I haven't added that to Tillie's duties yet. I'll have to make a note of it."

I got up to answer the door. It was Carol and her Mother Anita Richardson. They were both overdressed for a simple visit. Carol had a little red dress on while her Mother was showing off her body in a short tight baby blue sheath that left little to the imagination. Anita was carrying a small present that was wrapped in pink paper. She gave me a big smile.

"Carol told me that your Mother had a new maid. I wanted to see her for myself."

I knew I should have told Carol not to say anything to anybody but I never thought she would share Tillie with her Mother. That certainly explained their attire. Mom wasn't the only one who could tease. There was nothing that I could do about it now so I just invited them in. I let Mom know they were there and Mom followed the three of us into the sitting room.

I felt out of place. I was in my jeans while the three ladies all wore attire more suitable for an evening out. They presented a sultry image posed on the sofa with their legs crossed in a display of tempting femininity. There was a distinct fragrance of feminine perfume.

Anita handed the package to my Mother.

"I brought you a present Alicia."

Mom quickly unwrapped the small box. It was a little hand bell — the kind that is used to summon a servant. Mom beamed with approval while Anita smiled proudly.

"I thought you might need that. One little ring of the bell and your Tillie will come running."

"Absolutely perfect!"

I couldn't believe it. They wanted Tillie to respond to a bell like a hired servant! Anita was so excited she pressed Mom for more.

"Tell me all about Tillie."

"Well Tillie is a submissive sissy girl and she just *loves* to tend to household duties. I have her tending to my bathroom even now. She is such a prissy thing that she'll do anything for a woman. All I have to do is order her about and she obeys everything I say. I don't believe that I'll ever do any housework ever again. Natalie go fetch Tillie so that Anita can see for herself."

Anita nodded her head.

"When she gets here I can teach her how the bell works."

CHAPTER 11. *Servant's Bell*

Anita spoke to Tillie in a condescending manner like she was speaking to a child. She held up the little bell and gave it a tinkle.

"Tillie when you hear the bell that means that you are being summoned. Whatever you are doing is far less important than seeing to the needs of your uppers so you are to stop what you are doing and report immediately. Do you understand me girl?"

"I'm to respond to a bell? Like a servant?"

"Yes that's the idea dear."

"Yes Madam Richardson."

"When you report you are to say *Yes Madam may I help you* and then wait for further instructions. Do you understand?

"Yes Madam Richardson."

"Oh Alicia you've trained her so well!"

Carol couldn't help herself. She held her hand over her mouth while she giggled. If there was any virile male left in Tillie watching her take instructions from Anita Richardson extinguished it for good.

"Now back to work dear we'll ring for you if we need you. You are dismissed."

"Yes Madam Richardson."

Mercifully Tillie left the room and went back to work. The ladies laughed at the humiliation that had just been heaped upon the timid maid by — of all things —a visitor to our home.

But Anita wasn't done just yet.

"Alicia the girl's uniform is nice but have you considered something a bit more appropriate for a sissy girl?"

"What did you have in mind?"

"I was thinking a French maid would be more appropriate. You know, it would be more feminine."

I couldn't take it any longer. Before Mom answered I motioned to Carol and we both left the room. We went into Mom's office and I closed the door.

52

"Did you have to tell your Mother about Tillie?"

"I'm so sorry. It just sort of slipped out. Mom thought it was adorable and she had to see for herself. It is kind of funny."

"What is funny?"

"That your Mom turned your fiancée into her maid—of course."

"Tillie is not my fiancée. I never said yes. I don't think that's so funny either. If Mom disapproved of Tillie—I mean Timothy—she could have just said so. She didn't have to humiliate him."

"She isn't disapproving of him. She just likes having maid service. You don't approve of maid service?"

"Of course I approve. But if I wanted Tillie to be my maid I would have liked to have trained her myself. I mean for heaven's sake Tillie is hand washing Mom's panties for her. After that how can I possibly marry her, I mean him, I mean…"

"Take a deep breath Natalie."

"You know what I mean. It's embarrassing that Tillie allowed has herself to be dominated like that by my Mother."

Carol smiled.

"I see what you're saying. I guess that if you don't want Tillie anymore you can always send her over to my place. I like maid service!"

"Carol!"

CHAPTER 12. Formality

Things were even worse when we went back to the sitting room. Anita was still talking to Mom about Tillie. At least the maid was nowhere to be found.

"Something is missing Alicia. I think I know what it is. Summon the girl with the bell."

Mom lifted the bell and with a devious smile gave it a little tinkle. In seconds Tillie was standing in front of Mom.

"Yes Madam may I help you?"

I was embarrassed for Tillie but I hadn't seen anything yet. Anita picked it up from there.

"I think Tillie that things aren't quite formal enough just yet. If you are going to be a maid then you should be a proper maid. When you are summoned with the bell before you say *Yes Madam may I help you* I think that a little curtsy is in order. Don't you agree Alicia?"

Mom couldn't have been more agreeable. She quickly nodded her approval and then Anita began giving curtsy lessons to Tillie.

"Gently take the hem of your dress and then take a dainty dip. Yes, just like that. Now try it again only this time lift your hem a bit more like a good girl. That's too much dear. You aren't supposed to show so much of your panties.

Try it again. That's better. There you have it perfectly. Now you are dismissed girl and don't forget to curtsy from now on."

Tillie gave another curtsy before she turned and went back to work. The total humiliation of Tillie was complete. Or at least I thought so.

CHAPTER 13. French Maid

The next week when Tillie reported for duty a brand new French maid uniform was waiting for her. I was in Mom's office with her when the French maid minced in on her stiletto heels fully attired like a flirty French tart. There was even a hint of cheap perfume that accompanied her. Mom was pleased with the full effect the tiny dress had on her maid. Her stocking tops were visible and when Mom had her do a little twirl to show off her outfit I noticed that a bit of her white rumba panties were also visible.

Tillie managed to make things worse for herself. She politely asked for permission to speak before she confessed that the newspaper she worked at had closed and that she was out of a job. Mom was actually joyous.

"Oh how wonderful Tillie! You can move in here into our extra bedroom and be my maid full time!"

The maid tried desperately to plead for mercy.

"Please Madam Deshay…"

"No need to thank me dear. Now off to work."

The sissy maid curtsied for us and then minced out of the office to resume her duties. Mom looked at me.

"Natalie I presume that the wedding is off."

"We were never engaged Mom."

"Tillie does make a fine maid doesn't she?"

A few minutes later she presented herself back at the office door. Apparently Tillie changed her mind about accepting a role as a fulltime maid. Mom noticed her immediately.

"Come in Tillie. What seems to be the problem?"

"Madam Deshay I just can't be your full time maid."

"Oh, why not? The position suits you dear."

"It's humiliating for me…"

"Oh my, we wouldn't want that now would we? Perhaps we can convince you that being a maid isn't all that humiliating and then you'll change your mind."

Mom opened the top drawer of her desk and pulled out a familiar wooden ping-pong paddle. I remembered the paddle from when Mom taught me how to discipline little boys.

When I was quite small my younger brother Stevie was always giving me trouble. That is up until the day that Mom had me spank him for the first time. She kept the paddle in her desk drawer for convenience when needed and on that memorable day she let me use it. I don't remember what Stevie did wrong that time but I do remember clearly the look on Stevie's face when Mom gave me the paddle and the instructions that came with it.

"Natalie sit on the chair and arrange your skirt neatly so you won't get it wrinkled. Very good girl. All disciplinary spankings are to be administered on the bare behind. When you get older you'll be able to lower his pants when your brother is over your lap. Today take them down for him first and then put him over your knees."

I felt so powerful at that moment. I still recall those first stirrings of womanhood when I took Stevie's pants down. He was far too fearful of Mom to protest so he just stood there while I dropped his drawers to his ankles and then positioned him over my lap.

"Now then strike him squarely on his bottom and don't spare the effort. That's right."

She continued to speak louder over the whack of the paddle and the childish protests of my little brother.

"Rapid succession gets the point across. It is best to lecture while you spank in order to improve future behavior. Harder Natalie, you want those tears to flow so that he remembers his lesson. Very good."

I remember my arm feeling tired when Stevie finally began sobbing. His bottom was a rosy red and he was still draped over my lap like the naughty little boy that he was. A brother has a whole new respect for his older sister when she is put in charge of his discipline. Mom told me that I was free to punish Stevie whenever I felt like he needed it. I applied the paddle to his bottom many times after that so he was always extremely respectful of me.

My absolute authority over Stevie led to me assigning my household chores to him. It wasn't long after that when I had him doing laundry for me and running the vacuum cleaner.

I suppose that I completely humiliated my little brother. Mom always said that spankings weren't about inflicting pain but rather were about changing behavior with purposeful humiliation.

I recalled the time that Carol and my friend Lisa came over to do homework. Carol and Lisa both went to the same private school that I did. It was right after school when they dropped in so all three of us were still in our school uniforms. Stevie didn't have any homework that day so he was in the laundry room starting a load of laundry.

Carol had a crush on Stevie — she still does — and she asked where he was. When I told her she couldn't believe that Stevie did laundry.

Of course I had to brag. I told them that I was in charge of Stevie and that he did all the household chores for me. I said that if he didn't obey me that I could spank him any time that I wanted.

They didn't believe me so I said that I would show them both. I called for Stevie and told him that he was disturbing us by making too much noise so that he had to be spanked.

Carol and Lisa then watched with interest while I lectured Stevie and pulled his pants down. After he was suitably positioned over my knees the girls giggled when the paddle landed and they continued to giggle while I repeatedly applied the paddle while lecturing Stevie for being too noisy. When I finally let Stevie up he was crying but like he was required to do after every spanking he apologized to all three of us for his behavior.

Carol then said that it looked like fun and she wanted to give it a try. So I gave her the paddle and in an instant Stevie was over Carol's lap. She scolded Stevie by saying that boys need to learn respect for girls and that all girls should be able to spank boys anytime that they wanted. She spanked much harder than I did so Stevie's bottom must have really been stinging.

Again Stevie apologized to us for his behavior before I ordered him back to work. We all had quite a thrill humiliating Stevie like that. He must have been thoroughly embarrassed to be disciplined in front of my friends while they laughed and giggled at his predicament.

All of those thoughts went through my mind after Mom gave me the paddle and I took Tillie over my knees. I found the thought of spanking my former boyfriend to be erotic and I'll admit that my panties moistened while I turned his bottom a deep red.

After that Tillie thanked me for taking the time to discipline her and then she agreed to stay on as Mom's permanent domestic maid.

CHAPTER 14. Tillie Bonnet

It was just a few days later when I came home from work to find Mrs. Richardson and Mom sitting and talking. Just when I walked in the room I was greeted with the sight of Tillie slowly pushing a vintage tea serving cart into the room.

Tillie was still wearing her French maid uniform. Mom had turned her into a ditzy looking blonde with long shoulder length curly hair. The maid was perched on tall stilettos that caused her to take tiny little steps and she was topped off with a lace cap that had ribbons that flowed in back to her shoulders. She was made up like a French tart straight from the seedy streets of Paris. The only thing that was missing from her total feminization was her engagement ring.

The maid paid no attention to me. Instead she was concentrating on serving the ladies their tea. When I approached Mom smiled.

"You came just in time Natalie. Would you care for tea?"

I nodded and sat down. How could I not? The scene was like watching a train wreck. I simply could not look away. Not that I wanted to!

Mom had taken great care to make Tillie look like a real woman. I couldn't help but notice the unmistakable fragrance of a lovely perfume. She had extra-long eye lashes that made her eyelids flutter with every blink, she wore extra-long nail extensions that were polished pink and most noticeably she boasted of an ample womanly bosom with prominent nipples that were quite visible through her satin uniform. They protruded right through the fabric in a most lewd fashion.

After we were all poured a cup Tillie waited for her instructions. After Mom took a sip she glanced at the maid.

"That will be all for now Tillie."

"Oui Mademoiselle"

Then the maid dipped a polite curtsey before rolling the tea cart back into the kitchen. I couldn't believe what I had just seen and heard.

"Mom what did you do to Tillie?"

"What do you mean dear?"

"I mean that she is acting like a real French maid."

"I didn't do anything dear. It was all Anita's idea really. She thought that a French maid would be more mysterious so she helped me turn Tillie into Miss Tillie Bonnet an actual French maid. She is even teaching her French so that she sounds authentic. All it took was a few swishes of a whipping cane and Tillie was extremely agreeable. The cane was Anita's idea too."

Mom smiled with a certain pride before she continued.

"Did you notice her bustline dear?"

"How could I not?"

"Anita thought a womanly bust with prominent nipples would be a nice touch. It shows how excited she is to serve."

"You even bought a tea cart?"

"Yes, she's practicing today for the tea party. I'm going to have all the ladies over next week so that I can show off my new maid. I'm sure that they will all be jealous and that I'll be the envy of all of them."

"But Mom, Tillie isn't a real maid. She isn't even a real woman."

"You could have fooled me dear. I think that she's quite convincing."

Anita nodded her head.

"Yes quite convincing. I'm sure the ladies will be impressed with your fancy new soubrette."

"Mom what happened to her engagement ring?"

"I had her take it off. Anita thought that she probably wouldn't want to scare any boys away with it."

The ladies laughed together.

CHAPTER 15. Party Time

Sure enough the following weekend all of Mom's friends assembled for the big tea party. If there was still any doubt in my mind about marrying Timothy the indignity of him serving Mom's friends dressed up like a French maid was more than enough to extinguish those thoughts forever.

I never realized that Mom had so many friends. Our home was filled with the sounds of women gossiping while I nervously waited for Tillie to make her appearance.

It was apparent that Mom intended to fully humiliate the maid when she gathered all of the ladies together to make an announcement. Anita stood triumphantly at her side while she made her speech.

"Ladies it is true that submissive males do exist and that with work they can be taught how to perform basic mundane household chores. For proof I would like you to greet my daughter's former suitor Miss Tillie Bonnet."

I couldn't believe that Mom introduced Tillie like that! I was *so* embarrassed I doubt that I would ever be able to look any of Mom's friends in the eye ever again. I could have crawled under a rug.

With that introduction Mom rang the tiny servant's bell. After a slight delay Tillie timidly came out of the kitchen slowly pushing the tea serving cart.

The group of ladies roared with laughter while poor Tillie entered the room. Tillie was attired in her French maid uniform making no mistake that she had been totally feminized. To punctuate her humiliating indignity the raucous laughter hit a new high when the sissy maid dipped her obligatory curtsy.

The ladies applauded and congratulations began to flow to Mom on how well she had trained the sissy maid. While Mom received her accolades the red faced maid began to serve the ladies their tea.

It was a loud boisterous party with great amusement provided at the expense of the hapless maid. I suppose that the ladies couldn't believe that a male could be stripped of his ego like that and then humbled so much by a woman but Mom had proved it possible.

I could barely muster the strength to watch what had become of Timothy but I couldn't divert my eyes. There was something strangely erotic watching the subjugation of a male for the amusement of so many women. I found a strange stirring occurring deep inside of me that said that I was enjoying the conquest just like all of the other ladies.

Tillie may have gotten off easier had she not managed to spill a spot of tea on the serving cart. Anita made great sport out of pointing out the mistake while insisting that the maid be punished for her sloppy work.

CHAPTER 16. Another Spanking

Much to the delight of the crowd of women Mom berated the maid for her performance while they giggled in amusement. Then Mom insisted that Tillie fetch her paddle. I knew what it was leading up to but by the reaction of the crowd they had no idea.

When Mom ordered Tillie over her knees there was an audible gasp at the actions of the obedient maid. Before the shock subsided Tillie's frilly panties were down and Mom was applying the paddle to the maid's bare bottom.

It was almost too much for the women to take. They screeched with hilarity and even began to count the smacks while the maid was humiliated in front of them beyond belief.

When the count reached twenty Tillie had a bottom that was a brilliant red. To the delight of the captivated audience Tillie was then banished to a corner to stand with her panties still down and her dress held up high for all to see her shame. The ladies applauded Mom for her effort.

Tillie remained in the corner while the party continued. It wasn't until the final guest had left that Mom rang the servant's bell to summon the maid. She told Tillie what a proper maid that she had been but that next time the ladies were invited over she expected perfection. Then Mom dismissed her. With a final curtsy Tillie's humiliating evening ended. I doubted that she would be able to comfortably sit for quite a long time.

Mom smiled at me while the maid walked away.

"I believe that I told you that crossdressing sissy girls are a different breed of male. If you recall I said that there were possibilities. That was quite impressive, wouldn't you agree?"

She gave a little giggle.

I couldn't think of a thing to say. I simply nodded my head in agreement.

CHAPTER 17. Clint Steele

You might think that after what had happened with maid Tillie Bonnet the French tart that I would give up dating forever. While I was tempted to do just that I must admit that Tillie was cute. The truth is that I enjoy male company sissy girl or not. I can't help it if Mom stole my guy and turned him into her sissy maid. I may have done the same had I been given the opportunity. Besides when I met Clint Steele I couldn't help myself. I was in the grocery store struggling separating shopping carts from each other when Clint came up and with no effort at all he pulled a cart free for me.

It wasn't his liberation of the grocery cart for my benefit that impressed me. To free it he had forced it apart from the unyielding grip of another cart. I think that they make the carts that way specifically to drive shoppers crazy with frustration.

Anyway Clint made no effort to daintily handle the problem by strategically separating them like I was trying unsuccessfully to do. Instead he man-handled the situation like only a physically tough male could. In the process of freeing the cart with his brute strength the cart that was holding my desired cart hostage was bent out of shape.

Yes the virile, muscular well-chiseled Clint Steele could do that. With his flowing blond hair, rippling muscles and gleaming white broad smile he was the powerful male dream of every girl everywhere. Having saved me from shopping cart hysteria like a true gentleman he accompanied me into the store. He even brought a couple of items down for me from high up on the shelf. I swear that every woman we passed swooned at the sight of him. Why wouldn't they?

So when he asked me for a date how could I possibly refuse such a perfect specimen of a guy? There's nothing wrong with a little bit of rebound dating. Males like Clint Steele define masculinity. He practically dripped testosterone. He was a male god among mere mortals. I best stop at that because a girl can get extremely hot just thinking about a guy like Clint Steele. I know that I do.

I gleefully keyed his name and address into my cell phone. Just in case he was kidding me I wanted to make sure that I could find him. I didn't want to seem too eager so I resisted the urge to take selfies with him. It was of course a lost opportunity that I regret to this day.

He was to meet me after work at the office for our first date. When he arrived on the second floor where Carol and I worked with a single rose in hand all the ladies took notice. There was a quiet murmur while they all tried to guess who he was there for.

Carol gaped with her mouth open at the ultimate vision of a female fantasy.

"I wonder who *that* is?"

"That's my date Carol. His name is Clint Steele."

"Oh my God you must be kidding me! The guy is built like Superman! Look at those muscles and that flat stomach. He must work out every day."

"He does. Actually he said he works out twice a day. He told me that he works out once before work and once after work. Before he joined the workforce he played football in college. Can't you tell?"

"Quarterback?"

"Of course."

"He can huddle and play with me any time he wants."

"Carol!"

"I wonder if his equipment…"

"Stop it! He's *mine*. Hands off!"

I could feel the eyes of all the office women on us when Clint presented me with my rose and we left together for our date.

I felt like a princess. It was the most wondrous evening ever. We dined in luxury and then we strolled through the park and laughed while we talked. I had never been in the park after dark because of everything I had heard about crime there from Mom. Some of it was possibly even true. But I had no fear. No one would dare touch me with Clint Steele at my side. He was a mountain of strength and power so nobody would have the nerve to even approach us.

I wished that Tillie could see me enjoying my time with Clint. There's nothing that makes a guy more jealous than seeing his girl laughing and giggling while with another guy!

It was the perfect date. He was the perfect well-mannered male. At least he was until he took me home that evening.

I normally don't kiss on the first date. I'm just not that kind of girl. I like to leave my suitors longing for more. Tillie took forever just to hold my hand and that was fine with me. Other boys never reached that third or fourth date when I would decide if I would actually allow them a sweet kiss. It would usually be only a peck on the cheek of course but it would be a kiss nonetheless.

Clint wasn't interested in my first date preference. When we reached that awkward moment on Mom's front porch Clint wasted no time. In the wink of an eye he used his brute strength to his advantage and I found myself bent over backwards with his tongue halfway down my throat. I suppose that a guy like Clint simply takes what he wants with no questions asked.

Had he not taken my breath away I may have resisted such a primitive assault. But I didn't. Why would I? After Tillie it was quite refreshing to have a real man take such an interest in me. My knees gave way on me but with a single hand he held me helplessly in position successfully keeping me from falling over backwards. He held me tight just like that unable to escape his grip until my body surrendered and I eagerly returned his kiss.

It was much more than that. My virgin body totally betrayed me. While our tongues intertwined my swollen nipples jutted out in lewd approval like never before. They actually hurt from erotic lust. While making an excellent case for going braless they struggled to escape their tight brassiere prison.

Deep inside butterflies gave way to a passionate plea of moistness all ready for the taking. My virginity was ready to surrender to whatever he might have had in mind and I hoped that he did. Mom always said that a girl is supposed to be coy and not easily give in to the touch of a rogue. But it didn't matter to me. For a few moments I was a willing harem girl in the hands of a virile sultan.

I was still panting when he stood me back up and then he walked away without saying a single word. What a heavenly kiss it had been! I could only dreamily watch his trim well sculpted body stride away into the night like a conquering hero. The only thing missing was his white horse.

I didn't know that Mom had been watching us on our porch security camera but she had been. When I walked breathlessly in the front door she was waiting for me.

"My, my Natalie. *That* was quite a kiss. *That* was quite a man."

"Mother!"

I have to say that sleep eluded me for quite a while that night. A girl should never be left in the condition that I was in when I settled into my bed. I tried to sooth my breasts with my fingers by softly caressing my nipples but it was of no use.

Finally in total capitulation to my desperate need my vibrating pleasure wand did what Clint had failed to do. It was the only relief that I could find. I had to restrain myself and hold back an orgasmic moan so that Mom didn't hear what I had done.

At least then I was able to go to sleep.

CHAPTER 18. Second Date

Naturally I had to go out again with Clint if only to show the girls in the office that I had found a real man and that I could keep his interest. I wanted to give Clint a special tease so this time I wore my tightest little black dress that showcased every curve on my body.

I intended to tempt him but of course not much more than that. I am after all a good girl. But good girls can have fun too. So I wore stockings instead of pantyhose so that he could get a glimpse of my stocking tops. That always did a great job of teasing my dates so I knew it would work on Clint. Combined with a pushup bra, stilettos and an extra dash of my best perfume I felt like I was an irresistible knockout. The bra gave me more of what I already had and the heels would make it easier for me to gaze into his eyes. The fragrance was guaranteed to be sweet temptation.

Carol took notice of my attire.

"Hot date with Clint again? I love the outfit. It screams slut."

"It does not."

"If that doesn't scream slut then I don't know what does. Unless it's that heavy makeup. Where did you get that look from? Did you copy it from a Sluts R Us catalog? Don't worry, if things don't work out with Clint you can always stand on a street corner downtown."

"Carol! I'll do no such thing!"

Carol gave me her knowing grin.

"Well I have to say that somehow I think that Natalie is expecting much more than dinner and a kiss tonight."

"No not at all. It's only our second date."

"I think the lady doth protest too much."

She giggled at my attempt to cover up my true motive. I didn't care what she thought. After all I was going out with Clint Steele!

Again there was an audible gasp from the ladies at work when Clint arrived. This time he presented me with a golden necklace. He made quite a show out of gently lifting my hair and clasping it around my neck. I was the envy of all the girls.

81

Once again I was wined and dined like a princess in the magical world of Clint Steele. Then we sauntered through the moonlit park again. This time after the park stroll Clint wanted to show me his apartment. Naturally— and without giving it much thought —I agreed to go with him. The prospect of an evening of making out with Clint in the privacy of his apartment was far too much for me to resist.

I had dated so many sissy boys I guess I forgot what less refined guys are thinking when they are out on a date. Clint was a perfect gentleman again until we got to his apartment. He closed the door behind us and then he bolted it shut. Then in a quick move he pulled me tight against his body with his muscular arms. Before I could protest his tongue was halfway down my throat again and while one iron arm gripped my waist his other hand fondled my buttocks.

It seemed pleasant enough but he had no intention of stopping there. I felt my dress being lifted up from behind until it was bunched up around my waist. I don't know how he managed to do it with one hand but in one quick move he ripped my thong panties right off.

Now with two hands cupping my bare buttocks he pulled me tight against his pelvis. It wasn't until I realized that what I felt through his trousers wasn't something in his pocket that I started to panic. All that stood between my previously well-guarded virginity and his fully erect rather substantial masculinity was a thin layer of his bulging trousers.

To answer Carol's question his equipment was certainly what a girl would expect from such a well-built masculine specimen. His manliness was definitely not in question. For a fleeting moment I wondered what would happen if he put it to good use. Then I came to my virgin senses. Not only wasn't I sure that I could take such a robust thrust I was saving myself for that special guy who one day would marry me!

CHAPTER 19. Uber Driver

I stood outside his apartment waiting for the Uber to arrive. Fortunately I had remembered to pull my dress back down before I went out into the evening air. I still felt a bit cool because I had left my panties behind in his apartment. After all they had been ripped from my body and were no longer of any use to me.

I laughed to myself. The panties were useless. That was most likely the same condition that I had left Clint's magnificent sex organ in. A quick knee to the groin can do that even to a guy like Clint Steele.

The Uber pulled up and I was happy to see a woman sitting behind the wheel. I hopped in and closed the door. She spoke first.

"A date with Clint Steele?"

"How did you know?"

"I could tell by your hair. It's a bit mussed. Not to mention your smeared makeup. The Wonderbra and the stilettos gave it away too. Plus I've been here many times before. There are guys who don't know the difference between yes and no. I guess Clint is one of those guys. Some weekends I just park here and wait for the call."

I knew I hadn't been the first but for crying out loud! I was just another in a long line of women Clint had dated and tried to feel up.

"Did he take you out to dinner and then through the park?"

"Yes he did…"

"That's the only move he has dear. It seems to work on all the girls. He's quite a physical specimen isn't he?"

"You can say that again."

She dropped me back home. Again Mother was waiting for me inside.

"How was your date dear?"

"Don't ask."

"That bad?"

"He tried but at least I wasn't raped."

"It's not very gentlemanly but real men will do that sometimes. A girl should be more careful."

"Thanks Mom, I needed that. Would you summon Tillie for me and have her pour me a bath? I need to soak for a while."

"Sure dear."

CHAPTER 20. Changes

After the disaster with Clint I swore off men forever. After considerable thought I came to the conclusion that Clint just wasn't my type. If I ever changed my mind — and I resolved that I never would — I would go out with a more genteel guy. I would have to date somebody more like Tillie only with a little less makeup.

When Carol asked me what had happened with Clint I told her every horrendous detail. Then in true Carol fashion she asked me for his phone number. Of course I didn't give it to her, but Carol is like that. She just had to ask.

Things started happening at work. I got a promotion and left Carol behind on the second floor when I got a fabulous corner office up on the fourth floor. I also decided that I didn't want Mom spying on my night life anymore so I moved out and into an apartment that I shared with Carol.

It was just after I moved in with Carol that she came home late on a Saturday night. I was curled up with my kindle reading a favorite book when she walked in.

I couldn't believe my eyes. Carol was a mess. Her normally perfect hair was frazzled, she had lipstick smeared on her face and her favorite little black dress was ripped open in front. Her adorable racy bra was showing. It was an adorable black lace Wonderbra that screamed sexy. I made a mental note to ask her later where she bought it.

"Carol what happened? Your dress is torn. You look like you were raped!"

"Funny that you should say that. It was close but not exactly."

"Your mother always said that the success of a woman's outfit is directly related to a man's desire to tear it off of her but I'm not sure that she meant that literally."

"Well then this little black dress died a hero. It was not only a big success it was also a fashionable triumph."

"I'll call the police. Who did you go out with?"

"Don't bother—it's all taken care of."

She gave me a coy smile.

"Oh did I mention that I went out with Clint Steele?"

"You didn't! I told you not to see him!"

"Well if you hadn't left your phone out I probably wouldn't have been tempted but I couldn't help myself. I had to stand up for you."

"For me?"

"That's right. I have pictures. Do you want to see them?"

Only Carol could take pictures during an attempted rape. Of course I *did* want to see them.

"I took them with my phone but let me get my tablet. They're already up in the cloud. You'll want to have a good look."

We sat down together on the loveseat with Carol holding the tablet between us.

"We had a lovely dinner date. Clint sure knows how to treat a girl for dinner. That walk in the park was divine."

"I know. He likes to do that."

"Then I suggested we go to his place."

"You didn't!"

"Of course I did. When we got there I suggested that we play strip poker. He really liked the idea."

"You played strip poker with Clint?"

"Sure, why not? I knew I would win."

"Usually when I play strip poker I try to lose, but Carol I sure wouldn't want to lose to Clint."

Carol smiled.

"I always try to lose at strip poker too but this was different. I had a better idea."

Only Carol would scheme at strip poker.

"He was so happy to play. He liked my attitude. He said that the last girl he dated had far too much starch in her panties for his taste."

"I did not!"

"You might want to work on your make-out manners Natalie. It would seem that you were

90

not quite up to standards. Anyway the rules were that the winner got to take photos of the loser. So here goes."

She swiped the tablet and the first photo came on the screen. I couldn't believe my eyes.

"Wow! He sure is well hung!"

"I thought so too. Look at those muscles and that taut stomach. Have you ever seen such a male specimen?"

"That's not what I was looking at but like I said before he sure has all the right equipment. I've never seen an erection like…"

She swiped the screen again.

"What a cute little ass. Did you pinch it?"

Carol smiled.

"Of course I did. Oh did I mention the other rule of the game?"

There was another swipe of the screen and a close-up of a very personal area.

"You shaved him down there?"

"That was the rule. The winner got to shave the loser. Nothing left of the lion's mane but stubble!"

We laughed together.

"That was when he lost control. It was just too much tease and denial for him to take. I guess poor little Clint couldn't restrain his hard-on in the presence of a *real* woman. That's when he tore my panties off and ripped my dress. He's really quite a kisser don't you think? Maybe too much tongue."

"Carol I hope you're not pregnant."

She giggled.

"Of course not. Let me show you the next picture and you'll see.

She swiped the screen again.

"Oh my gosh, he's doubled over in pain. What happened?"

"I kicked him right in the nuts."

"That seems to happen to him quite a lot."

"I was there for payback, not to play. So I taught him a lesson that he won't soon forget."

She touched the screen.

"Is he *outside* in that one — *naked*?"

I couldn't suppress a giggle.

"That's right. When I was going out the door and he was trying to recover from being turned into a soprano I mentioned that he had to be a real dumb jock to play strip poker with a deck of marked cards."

"You brought a deck of marked cards?"

"Of course. I wouldn't have prodded him into playing strip poker otherwise."

Fortunately there was an Uber parked right outside the apartment complex and I got in right before he got to the car."

The next photo was priceless.

"Here's Clint standing in the headlights pounding on the hood of the Uber. He sure looks angry doesn't he?"

"He's still naked!"

"Not to worry though."

"Why not?"

CHAPTER 21. Police Woman

There was more than a hint of excitement in Carol's voice.

"You know how there's never a cop around when you need one? Well it was my lucky day because right at that moment a squad car came around the corner."

The next picture was even better. Clint was bent over the hood of the car and the female police woman was cuffing a very angry but still naked Clint.

"Here is Officer Marcie handcuffing Clint. After that I got back out of the car. Then I decided to take video. This is the best part."

Carol started the video. Clint was still bent over the hood of the Uber car fully illuminated by the headlights of the squad car and the officer was standing in the background.

"Is she putting on gloves?"

"She said it was policy for doing the cavity search."

"You're freaking kidding me!"

"Really. She said searching for contraband is standard procedure under the circumstances. See. There she is applying the lubricant and checking deep inside for possible contraband."

I giggled. I couldn't help myself. The whole scene was riveting. I was absolutely glued to the video. The officer took off her gloves.

"Is she frisking him?"

"That's right. She said it was policy to frisk for hidden weapons."

"But he was naked!"

"I think that she noticed that but she frisked him anyway."

"What's she doing there? She's not…"

"She is! She said that she found a dangerous weapon and she had to disarm it…"

"She's *milking* him! Oh dear—that didn't take long! He spurted everywhere! I hope he didn't get any on you."

His magnificent manhood gushed semen before shrinking down to a mere shadow of its former glory.

"I was okay, he just missed my heels. These are good shoes you know. Anyway Officer Marcie noted that he had a possible premature ejaculation issue. She said she would put it in her report. She said the court likes to know that sort of thing so it all comes out in open court."

"Seriously?"

"Oh yeah. Marcie said they have a female judge who handles these cases and she likes to know all of the intimate details. So do the rest of the ladies on the force."

"What's Officer Marcie doing there?"

"She's collecting samples for the rape kit."

"But you weren't raped."

"Once that sample went into the rape kit I was. Evidence is evidence!"

We both laughed. Then I had a thought.

"I guess when the judge hears the case Clint will end up doing *hard* time."

We both laughed again.

"There's Clint being driven away in the squad car."

"He sure looks contrite."

"That's because he's still naked. Marcie said the girls at the precinct like to take pictures with their cell phones when naughty boys come in so she doesn't offer them anything to cover up with."

"Serves him right."

We both laughed.

"He won't be brought into court naked will he?"

"Of course not. But Marcie said that the judge doesn't show much mercy with this kind of crime. She said he'll be put into panties, a bra and a pink dress like the girls wear at the ladies correctional facility before he gets to court. The judge feels like if these perpetrators want to get into ladies clothes then they should be indulged. Marcie said once he is found guilty and sentenced he'll be spending his time in the ladies correctional facility dressed just like the other girls doing laundry for the female inmates."

"Perfect! But won't he complain to someone about his treatment? I mean he'll be totally humiliated."

"Do you really think that Clint Steele will admit that he was humiliated like that to anyone? I don't think so!"

"Of course you're right. He has no option except to submit and to take his feminized medicine. I just wish that I could see it for myself."

"By the way Camille said to say hello."

"Camille?"

"The Uber driver. She said to say hi. She had so much fun watching what happened to Clint that she didn't even charge me for the ride home. Can you believe it?"

"I think she waited a long time for that."

"Natalie do you think that the girls at the office would like to see these pictures?"

"Knowing them they'll probably want to put them on a commemorative mug."

She was right about that. The girls on the second floor turned the video into snapshots that circulated around the office for days. A photo of Clint spurting while being milked by Officer Marcie found its way onto coffee mugs all over the office with the caption *The Milkman Cometh*. Carol even offered me a mug but I turned her down. Somehow I couldn't imagine drinking coffee out of a mug like that.

The video *Police Woman Milks Stud* was uploaded to YouTube and quickly went viral. There were over 500,000 views by noon of that first day it was posted. One thing was absolutely certain. Clint Steele was sure to remain the butt of jokes among women for months to come.

CHAPTER 22. Dean Livingstone

It was going to be a great day. Human Resources was dropping by with my new administrative assistant and they were scheduled to arrive at any minute. I was looking forward to the help that an eager young female assistant would bring for me.

It was an unusual situation. I held the corner office on the fourth floor but I was the only employee working there. The top executives were housed up on the sixth floor in the luxury suites. Floors one thru three were filled but there wasn't room for me down there on three. So I was the first person up on four. When business slowed down I was left as the only occupant and it had been that way for months. So I was thrilled to be finally getting company.

I was so excited that I stood by the elevator at precisely the moment that they said they would be there. You could imagine my surprise when Miss Baldwin from personnel stepped out of the elevator along with our new recruit — one Dean Livingstone.

The surprise wasn't that my administrative assistant was male — though I was expecting a

young lady. No the surprise was that I knew
Dean from my school days. You might say that I
knew him rather intimately in fact.

We all have secrets from our youth. There are
things that we did back then that affect us for our
whole life that we would rather not mention. For
me Dean was one of those relationships that I
never spoke about. When I was in school I knew
a boy named Dean Livingstone and he was my
secret lover.

Watching the slim newcomer with his fine
features come out of the elevator instantly
transported me back in time. He was still a blue-
eyed angel who could cause my heart to pick up
the pace. He still had the same boyish looks with
the same sandy hair and the same charming
smile that could easily win over any girl he
decided to have.

I met Dean in school when I was just a little girl
still in search of her precious first kiss. Dean sat
one row over from me and a couple of seats up
right in front of my best friend Carol Richardson.
I had a crush on Dean, along with several other
boys, so I had been watching him closely all
semester.

From the way he was sitting I could see his underwear when he would tuck his shirt in. A girl notices such things.

We were really just children back then so on that school day when I noticed something unusual about Dean I didn't hesitate to rather casually point it out. It was the least I could do given the humiliation that I knew it would bring him and the attention that I would garner. I couldn't help myself so when we were out for recess I came up to Dean.

"I know what you're wearing."

Truth be told I had only gotten a quick glimpse of his underwear and I really wasn't absolutely certain that I had seen panties. It was just a guess and a lucky one at that. But he didn't know that and so it was the way he reacted that confirmed my suspicion.

He knew exactly what I was referring to. His face blushed a little like only a young boy can blush and he immediately became defensive.

"What are you talking about?"

"You know. *Panties*. You're wearing girl's *panties*."

103

That faint blush on his cheeks turned a dark red.

"I am *not*."

"You are too. I saw them."

"I'm not wearing panties."

I knew I had him right where I wanted him. Visions of my first kiss danced in my head.

"I'm going to tell *all* the girls that you're wearing panties just like we do unless…"

He was too eager for his own good. Boys are like that. The idea of total humiliation in front of all of the girls in the school was just too much for him to imagine. He could never possibly live down such humiliation and he knew it. I tried to remain coy.

"Unless what?"

I paused for a moment. I wanted to make sure that I could get everything that I wanted.

"Unless you meet me in the secret place right after school."

The secret place was a hidden alcove right behind the school conveniently tucked between the gym and the hallway that led to the library. There were no windows there and it backed up to secluded woods. Teachers didn't go there so it was a perfect hiding place for students to go unobserved. Many of the girls had enjoyed their first kiss in that very spot so it was legendary among us and we had all had heard delightful stories about it and the joy that it could bring.

I guess Dean suspected what was going to happen to him back there so he wasn't ready to agree to my terms. But he really had little choice in the matter. I only allowed him a moment to hesitate before I prodded him along. Sometimes a girl has to do that.

"It doesn't matter to me. I'm sure that Carol and all my other friends would love to hear about your pretty panties."

They were in fact pretty. I had seen the tiny white waist band and a bit of the little red roses that decorated the white nylon fabric. In fact I owned a pair just like it.

I mentioned Carol because everybody knew that she liked to gossip. Telling Carol something like a scoop on a boy wearing panties was just like making an announcement over the school public address system.

Dean knew that too. So he agreed to meet me in the secret place right after school.

CHAPTER 23. First Kiss

When I arrived in the secret place Dean was
already nervously waiting for me there. Classes
had ended and all of the students had gone
home. The busses had long since left and the
grounds were silent except for the chirping of the
birds from the nearby woods.

I knew that I had Dean right where I wanted him
and I knew that it was a golden opportunity to
take advantage of the situation. Even at that age I
knew better than to let good fortune like that get
away from me. I playfully approached him in the
hidden alcove with a big smile on my face.

"So tell me Dean, how did you manage to find
yourself wearing a pair of girl's panties to
school?"

He was clearly uncomfortable with the question
but of course he knew he had to answer
truthfully.

"Mom forgot to wash whites this weekend so I
had to wear a pair of my sister's panties."

I giggled at the embarrassing revelation that
made him so uncomfortable. I suppose I could

have left it at that but it wasn't often that I had
the opportunity to get the better of a boy. At that
age the boys were always teasing the girls. My
bra had been snapped on more than one occasion
and boys were always trying to look up my skirt.
There wasn't much that I had been able to do
about it. This was *my* opportunity to have some
fun.

"We need to do a panty check. Undo your pants
so I can get a good look."

I would not have expected him to do that. I was
just fishing to see how he might respond but to
my surprise his trembling hands undid his pants
and he opened them up slightly. Then he spread
his shirttails apart and revealed a lovely pair of
girl's panties. They were precisely the pair that I
thought they were—white nylon with a pretty
red rose pattern. In retrospect it was a fine choice
for the first pair of panties for a sissy boy.

His eyes looked longingly for mercy. I slowly
came closer and with one finger I pulled the
waistband and gave it a quick snap. It was the
least that I could do to show my female
superiority.

"Those are very pretty panties Dean. I have a
pair just like them."

With that I gave him a quick kiss on the lips. It was the first time I had ever kissed a boy. His mouth opened in surprise and in a delightful moment of pure exploitation of the situation my second kiss was open mouth and all tongue.

"Meet me here again tomorrow after school and you had better be wearing panties."

With that I turned and triumphantly ran all the way home.

CHAPTER 24. *Just A Kiss*

I suppose most girls would have just left it at that. But when Dean showed up the next day wearing a different pair of panties—pink nylon with yellow daisies— visions of making out with him danced in my head. A kiss is just a kiss but at that age making out with a boy is what little girl dreams are made of.

So for Dean the price of my continued silence was that he had to come by my house so that we could do homework together after school. After all, we *had* to do homework and there were days when Mom came home from work late and my brother Stevie would be outside playing with his friends. It was my chance to be alone with Dean and I wasn't about to let it get away.

Once Mom met Dean she judged him safe to be in the house with me. I guess his angelic blue eyes worked on her too. Mom had always warned me about mischievous boys disguised as angelic boys. She said they had a way of seducing pretty girls like me. Perhaps she should have heeded her own advice. I think that she must have fallen for him too because after all she did decide that he was safe.

We would go into the basement playroom together to do our homework so that we were out of Mom's way. Little did she know that the first thing I did when we were alone was to do a panty check on Dean followed up with a deep French kiss. Or maybe she did know. After all she was a young girl once too.

It wasn't long before I gave Dean some of my panties to wear. I didn't want his Mother or Sister to get wind of what he was doing. After all, why spoil my fun? To throw them off he put his guy underwear in the wash every day at home and then he would bring his worn panties over with him to visit. I showed him how to hand wash his panties and then hang them up to dry while we did our homework.

One thing led to another. That year kissing led to groping which led to heavy petting. They were all firsts for me. I'm absolutely certain that had Dean's family not moved to a different school district that I wouldn't have remained a virgin very much longer. We were young but we were rapidly discovering the pleasures of each other's company and it wouldn't have taken much longer for us to decipher how our intimate parts fit together.

Instead I teased Dean unmercifully but naturally I denied him complete satisfaction. His constant state of arousal kept him interested in me. I suppose you could say that I kept my blue-eyed angel in a constant state of blue balls. It was all for his own good. Dean didn't seem to have much objection to any of it.

To be sure I thought of myself to be a pretty good tease. I enjoyed every minute of driving Dean crazy with desire for me. It was with Dean Livingstone that I learned how to successfully flirt with boys.

I never told anyone about Dean except for of course Carol. I tell Carol everything. Even though she promised to keep it a secret like always she didn't keep it a secret for very long. She shared my story with all the girls at school and they all had a good laugh at Dean's expense. Even at that age we could appreciate the amusement of a boy wearing panties.

Once Dean moved away I hadn't seen him again. At least not until that morning when he stepped out of the elevator and back into my life.

CHAPTER 25. Professionals

To our credit for that first week we both tried to remain totally professional. We both pretended that Dean was just my assistant and that we had no past together. Out of respect for my position of authority he even called me Miss Deshay instead of Natalie. But in retrospect I suppose given that we were alone up on the fourth floor it was only a matter of time before things got out of hand.

It all came to a head on an evening when I was working late with Dean. The building was empty. Even Carol, who worked down on two and typically went home with me, had left for the day. We were both tired and ready to call it a day. Dean was sitting in front of my desk and our eyes met and locked. I could see that his mind was where it shouldn't be. I felt myself melting into his gaze.

"Dean we shouldn't…"

"I know but…"

"No Dean. We aren't children anymore."

"Maybe for old time sake…Just once…"

I couldn't take it any longer. I could see that he was going to be persistent.

"Okay stand up Dean. You're long overdue for a panty check."

He smiled that enchanting smile and stood up. Without hesitation he undid his trousers and parted his shirttails to reveal a lovely pair of pink panties with a tiny little red rose pattern. I couldn't help myself. I burst out laughing.

"I have to admit Dean your taste in panties is still very good."

His face flushed.

"Thank you Miss Deshay."

"Have you been wearing panties all of these years?"

He shook his head.

"Tell me all about it."

Dean stood there with his panties showing while he spoke.

"I've never told anyone about us or about my panties. It's been my secret all of these years."

"Mine too."

Okay, a girl can lie just a little can't she?

"I love the feel of panties and I think about you every day when I pull them on."

Oh great I thought, a lovesick sissy boy pining away for me all those years. It was a great line. It was clever and more than enough to melt a girl's heart.

Before I go any further I want to make it clear that even then I suspected that Dean was really a devilish boy disguised as an angel. But at the time it didn't matter to me. If he was being devious it was okay because what followed was worth it. He was delightful.

A light kiss led to a deep French kiss. Then we were in the employee lounge making out on the couch. Mind you we just kissed and held each other. It was a perfect tease and denial session that left us both wanting for more.

I knew that there was a company policy that forbids such things. We could both be fired for just having that first make-out session. Perhaps it was that clandestine requirement that titillated something deep inside and intensified my arousal. Anyway we agreed that we had to see more of each other and that it had to be kept a deep dark secret.

So we made rules to avoid suspicion. We would only meet on Monday, Wednesday and Friday. Dean would be one of the last to leave the building and he would go across the street to the diner and order carry-out. Then he would return and we would have a slow private dinner in the employee lounge still attired in our office clothes. After that we would kiss and make out in prolonged forbidden lust before leaving the building separately. To avoid suspicion, of course.

Mind you that Dean conducted himself like a sort of perfect gentleman. While he would kiss and fondle me he never tried to have intercourse with me. He never even tried to remove my panties. Instead we would tease and deny each other just like back at the schoolyard. I would leave for the evening with my panties moist from yearning lust.

I knew where it was leading. He was seducing me in a prolonged dance that could only end one way. Or so I thought. I was still a virtuous virgin but I wanted to give myself to him. I even started wearing stockings instead of pantyhose because I wanted to make it easier for him when he decided that the time was right.

CHAPTER 26. Secrets

Of course I couldn't tell Carol anything about our secret rendezvous. I never even told her that Dean was working for me. She never could keep a secret and if she spilled the beans I would be unemployed.

If I told Carol that Dean was my new assistant I knew that she would have ideas about how I should handle him. I could just hear her if I told her about my new assistant.

"Dean Livingstone? You mean the boy that you put in panties back in grade school? I remember that he was sooo cute! But if he's still wearing panties he must really be a wimp."

"I think that he has a crush on me."

"Of course he does. You're jaw dropping gorgeous just like me. Why wouldn't he have a crush on you? That doesn't mean that you can't have some fun with him. Bring him by and I'll show you what we can do with that kind of sissy girl."

Of course I wouldn't pay any attention to Carol even if she knew. She always has crazy ideas about what to do with boys and I didn't want her to interfere with my new love.

So I didn't tell Carol about Dean. It worked out. At just about the same time she started seeing someone. After that we never seemed to meet after work so we didn't have a chance to speak about my fresh squeeze. Our paths simply didn't cross. I would be in bed before she came home and she would be in bed before I came home. It was all for the better.

Things became serious with Dean. I could tell that Dean was going to be the love of my life. He was my first crush and he would be my last. I would willingly give my virginity to him. Date after date he practiced the art of slow seduction. He drove me wild with lust but I kept my panties on while he stroked and teased me. My body ached for him in a way I had never felt before.

For heaven's sake a girl can only wait so long! At a certain point in her life a girl has to have something between her legs that doesn't run on batteries. Just when I was at the point of begging him to rape me he produced what he called a friendship ring that he said was a promise of more pleasurable things to come.

It was a beautiful antique appearing blue sapphire ring that he said had belonged to his grandmother. The blue stone was surrounded by little white diamonds. My heart just melted. He cupped my buttocks and gave me a deep French kiss that I shall never forget. Just when I was ready to rip his pants off in uncontrollable lust he said that he wanted the evening to be memorable for something other than a make out session. So he went home early without any further affection.

The excitement was far too much for me not to share. Since it was still early I burst into the apartment to find that Carol was still up. With all of my pent up excitement I rambled on about my secret love while she carefully listened with a glow of sweet satisfaction that only a perfect friendship could provide.

She was so happy for me. Until I showed her the ring that Dean had given me just moments before. Her face fell into a concerned frown.

"Did he say it belonged to his grandmother?"

"Why yes."

"Wait a minute."

She went back into her bedroom and in just a few moments she came back to me. With a stern look on her face she held out a ring—an identical blue sapphire ring complete with white diamonds surrounding the center stone. We held the two rings together to be sure. They glistened in the light as though they were both brand new.

"Natalie, what is the name of your secret admirer?"

"I can't say."

I demanded the same from her.

"What's the name of *your* secret admirer?"

"I can't say either."

"It wouldn't be someone from work would it?"

It hit us both at the same time like a ton of bricks. We both spoke in unison.

"Dean Livingstone!"

We both threw our rings to the floor at the same time. When they hit the tile floor they both shattered into tiny bits of glass. Grandmother's antique ring my ass! They were worthless fake glass jewelry probably bought at a discount junk jewelry store. What a cheap douchebag!

Trust me--we were both embarrassed beyond belief. We had both fallen for the same ploy at the same time. I never felt so humiliated in my life. How dare him do that to us!

CHAPTER 27. Plotting

It would have never occurred to us that we were
both seeing the same boy but it made sense.
Carol only dated on Tuesday, Thursday and
Saturday while I was dating on Monday,
Wednesday and Friday. The pervert was two
timing us in a kind of perverse payback for what
we had done to him back in school.

We shared intimate details. Carol had also been
unmercifully teased and denied by the bastard.
Just like with me he would bring her right to the
brink and then send her home with moist panties
all ready for the delightful thrust of a male rod
that would never come. We realized that it was
all strictly a payback for leaving him all those
years ago with a bad case of blue balls and with
an irresistible panty fetish. We had been taken
for a sexual thrill ride that wasn't going to ever
end while he was laughing at us behind our back!

To say that we were angry would be a gross
understatement. I wanted to kick him in the balls
and never see him again. Carol had even better
ideas. What Dean didn't know was that Carol
and I were still best of friends and that we shared
the same apartment. Now it was our turn for
paybacks.

For a conniving douchebag Dean wasn't very bright. On her next Saturday date with Dean Carol insisted that he come to her apartment to meet her roommate. Perhaps visions of a three-way danced in his naughty head but for whatever reason he fell right into our trap.

After Carol brought him into our apartment I made a grand entrance. The look on his face was priceless. Had I been thinking I would have taken a photo for posterity in order to share the moment with all my friends at work.

He immediately realized how much trouble he was in. After the shock wore off he produced his cell phone from his pocket.

"Ladies before you say a word I want you both to know that I have pictures of you both back at the office in uncompromising positions. With one push of a button I can put you both in the unemployment line."

He was right about that. I knew that I shouldn't have posed topless for him but he had teased my nipples into such lovely swollen buds that I hadn't been able to refuse him. I surmised that he had one the same with Carol. I do have standards but it was so difficult to resist his

124

seduction so without thinking I had dropped my top for his photo op.

Fortunately Carol *was* thinking. In one swift move she snatched his phone from his hand.

"Did you say that you have pictures of us in here and that you plan to blackmail us?"

He was so smug it was sickening.

"Yes, I believe you get the picture."

He chuckled at the poor pun.

"Just on this very camera with no back up?"

His smile turned to a frown. It was a perfect gotcha moment. Then in an angry gesture Carol spiked the phone to the floor and used her heel to grind it into several pieces.

"Oops, I dropped it. I do hope that you have insurance on that thing."

"That phone was worth…"

"Shut up!"

With that Carol slapped him across his face. He gave her a stunned look. I thought it might be fun to do the same to him so I also gave him a firm slap on the other cheek.

Carol decided to put the rest of our plan into action. She gave him her very best gotcha smile.

"Time for a panty check Dean."

CHAPTER 28. Maid For Us

From that point on it was easy. That evening he was wearing purple nylon panties with little pink roses. For him it would just be a start of things to come. Carol ordered him to strip out of his clothes while I took pictures of him standing in just his pretty panties.

Then Carol had him wait while she rummaged about in her bedroom. When she came back out holding feminine clothing his eyes widened. Carol knew he couldn't resist so she was determined to play on his weakness for feminine attire.

When she presented him with a bra she didn't even have to order him to put it on. He quickly clipped it on like a good sissy girl. Garter and stockings followed before Carol padded out the bra cups with a couple of pairs of old pantyhose.

With the addition of a plain white slip Dean was ready for the grand finale. Carol had an old waitress uniform that she had worn at a previous job. She held it out for him and told him to put it on.

With his hands trembling the little turd took it. I couldn't believe it—he was turned on by the humiliation. That wasn't exactly what we had in mind so we both knew that we would have to do better than that.

It had all been *too* easy. While the new maid cleaned house, served dinner and eventually poured Carol a bath it became evident that Dean was enjoying himself. Even when Carol started calling him Deanna and referring to him as *she* and *her* he didn't seem terribly upset.

By the end of the weekend it was clear that turning Deanna into our live-in housemaid hadn't been much of a payback for what had been done to us. Being dominated by two gorgeous women like us apparently was erotic for Deanna. Perhaps it was because of what I had done so many years ago with her. It wasn't until late Sunday that Carol came up with an even better idea.

CHAPTER 29. Personal assistant

"Natalie I think I know how we can really humiliate Deanna."

"I'm glad you've thought of something because this sissy maid routine isn't getting the job done. I think Deanna is just enjoying herself."

"Since you were expecting a female assistant why don't we have Deanna become your assistant?"

I thought about it for a moment.

"You mean have her come to work dressed up like my female secretary?"

"Why not?"

It made sense. I was the only one working up on the fourth floor and I hadn't seen Miss Baldwin from human resources since Dean reported for work. So I could do whatever I wanted with Deanna and nobody would be the wiser. Of course no doubt Deanna would squirm with humiliation fearing discovery that could come at any minute. It was perfect.

We agreed that Deanna would be my personal office assistant by day and our live-in maid by night. So that Monday we put our plan into action.

Once Deanna realized what we were doing she was extremely reticent. Carol insisted that Deanna have a sexy secretary persona so we bought her generous falsies and put her in sexy lingerie and a short tight skirt suit that displayed every alluring padded out curve on her body. Her curly wig and soft pink makeup gave her an innocent sex appeal that would make her a sure target for any single male who happened by. With a pair of sexy open toe heels, plenty of bling and far too much of a musky perfume she was ready to report to work.

The idea achieved the desired effect. When we arrived at the office my new assistant meekly slinked across the lobby towards the elevators with flushed pink cheeks. Her heels clicked along the tile floor just like she was one of the girls. A few of the guys hungrily eyed her while she attempted to go unnoticed. When we reached the elevators Deanna couldn't get in to the elevator to the fourth floor fast enough before finally relaxing in the solitude of the lift. At last we had the revenge that we were looking for.

The idea was to continue to humiliate Deanna for a week or so while she learned her lesson and then she would return to being Dean. It would have been a rousing success except at the end of the week Miss Baldwin from human resources stopped by to let me know that more offices were going to be moved to the fourth floor on Monday.

CHAPTER 30. Changes

Miss Baldwin stood in my office looking out at my female personal assistant.

"Natalie, who is that at Dean's desk and where is Dean?"

You have to understand that I had to think fast. So I came up with the best response that I could.

"Miss Baldwin that is Deanna. Dean is, well, going through a change and part of her pre-op…"

She held her hand up to stop me mid-sentence and gave me a little giggle.

"I've heard of that! Boys becoming girls. Isn't that *so* sweet? Of course we'll accommodate her and make her feel at home. I'll even get her a new nameplate as soon as possible. It's the least we can do for her."

When she left my office she smiled at Deanna.

"I love your outfit. You look very cute young lady."

Deanna flushed a deep dark red.

That weekend Deanna tried to talk us out of her office dress code but we would have no part of it. That next Monday morning when the movers began bringing furniture in for the new employees Deanna was at her desk looking like an enticing little tart.

The movers noticed her outfit and several of them began hitting on her. Deanna was completely flustered by all the attention. She tried to take refuge in my office but I could see that when she got up from her desk that drew even more attention from the guys.

"Natalie they're hitting on me!"

"Try not to give them that come hither look dear."

"I was doing no such thing!"

"Well dressed the way that you are all it says is come hither."

I gave a little laugh. Paybacks can be so much fun!

The next day four more offices were moved up to the fourth floor. Deanna had a new nameplate on her desk proudly describing her as Miss Deanna Livingstone—Personal Assistant. The other assistants all introduced themselves to her and that is how she became a permanent female assistant.

CHAPTER 31. Even Better

Carol and I were satisfied with the job we had done with Deanna. Not only did we have her working like a maid in our apartment but we had the satisfaction of sending her off to work every day dressed like the office tart.

Meanwhile down on the second floor the ladies had all heard about the pre-op sissy up on the fourth floor. Carol said that Deanna was the topic of conversation in the lunch room so there was no way that she could ever go back to being Dean and still save face.

That would have been the end of her humiliation except Carol's aunt Mildred and her cousin Simone dropped by our apartment unannounced to visit us. Of course they were both impressed that we could afford to have maid service in our apartment. Mildred fawned over Deanna while Simone also wholeheartedly approved of our domestic help.

Simone took Carol aside while I talked with Mildred. Apparently she asked how much we were paying our maid. That was when Carol disclosed to her cousin that Deanna was in fact a submissive sissy maid. Simone was genuinely

135

interested in how she could get a sissy maid of her own. Carol said that she didn't think that Aunt Mildred would understand so they would have to talk about it another time when Aunt Mildred wasn't present.

After that brief introduction Simone talked about Deanna with her college friends. Once she shared the experience with them naturally they wanted to know more about sissy maids. So Simone asked Carol if she would be willing to talk to a few of them.

It was after that inquiry that Carol had another idea. Since we had already totally humiliated Deanna why not teach her how to have more respect for women? So Carol called Simone back and that was how we arranged to have little seminars for her college friends so they could experience first-hand how to dominate a submissive male.

At least the sessions started out small. All of them were held at our apartment and at our first seminar only Simone and two other young college coeds were present.

We began with a short lecture that Carol gave telling the girls that women of all ages are superior to males. Then she expounded the virtues of the submissive male and how to earn their adulation with our sexuality. Then she went on to teach the finer points of teaching sissy maid behavior.

That first group was both naïve and shy. They had no idea what a submissive male was and they had certainly never heard of a sissy maid before. When Carol finished her lecture and I summoned Deanna with the serving bell the girls appeared shocked when they saw her and all they could manage were nervous giggles.

Deanna slowly appeared pushing a little vintage serving cart. I could see the humiliation of serving strange young ladies heaping down on the sissy maid. She was so adorable when she was being humbled in that fashion. Then in a final loss of any remaining dignity she may had left she poured drinks and served snacks to the astounded coeds. It was the most delightful scene I could ever imagine. It was the start of greater things to come.

CHAPTER 32. Seminar

What sort of things did we teach at our sissy maid seminars? We liked to teach the basics about the essential aspects of petticoat discipline in a loving female led relationship.

The submissive male is different than the typical male. These males relate to women like role models while looking up to us and adoring us. They are most interested in pleasing the woman in their life and will do so whenever given the opportunity.

When taking control of a submissive male an authoritative woman is committing to managing her relationship with her male. She is deciding to instill a regimented system of tutoring used to not only control but also readjust traditional male behavior and typical male thinking.

We stressed that an authoritative woman can train such a male to her personal liking simply by using repetitive learning practices. The task of taking full charge is best accomplished and reinforced by demanding the submissive male wear attire normally reserved for servile women.

The concept is to bring front and center for the submissive male a realization of their own inferiority to women in general and specifically to the woman in their lives. Typically a submissive male deep down already understands his place on the social ladder but only subconsciously. This conscience realization brought home with the use of a maid uniform ensures that they understand and always keep their proper place in the relationship.

Reinforcement of such understanding with feminine clothing and appropriate discipline measures when needed encourages their docility and submissiveness. Most importantly males trained in this manner learn how to properly respect women, defer to women and how to properly obey women.

The use of a maid uniform is important in this process. To impress upon the submissive male his new position the clothes that they are required to wear should always be the same kind that a female of a low status would wear. For instance the clothing of a young school girl would also be acceptable during the training period. Of course in most cases the commonly selected attire is that of a maidservant.

Wearing the clothing of a maidservant promotes the mindset of a maidservant. Soon the submissive male finds himself engrossed in the role of what is commonly called a sissy maid.

Since most of the attendees of our seminars were unfamiliar with sissy maids we always offered a definition. For the uninitiated a sissy maid is a submissive male who wears female clothing and has been trained by a woman to act like a female for the benefit of an actual female. In these cases the woman in charge is often but not always referred to as their Mistress. Other typical terms for the lady in charge are Miss, Madam and ever Her Ladyship. Once appropriately trained the feminized sissy maid finds herself absorbed in common household tasks along with other services specified by her Mistress that are typically assigned to a domestic ladies maid. These services may include things like assistance dressing, assistance bathing and even daily application of makeup along with hair styling.

With the need to give pleasure to a woman fully satisfied the sissy maid remains absorbed in her work while the Mistress enjoys the pleasures that only being Mistress of the Manor can bring. Much to the joy of the Mistress typically the pleasure the sissy maid receives from servitude keeps her fully wrapped up in her new position of loyal servant. Thus the sissy maid is unable to do anything other than occupy herself in the role of maidservant.

We also explained that these relationships can be wife/husband, girlfriend/boyfriend or even a platonic relationship between a woman and her maid. The important point is that the authoritative woman receives the pleasures of maid service while the submissive sissy maid satisfies her own innate desire to serve. It is a most charming quid pro quo on the highest level.

Attendees to our seminars often asked how such behavior could possibly be enforced. Our answer was to explain that under these circumstances the lady in control may be compelled to take appropriate measures to ensure her imperial rule remained intact.

We stressed that it does not take a total breakdown of servitude to inspire a Mistress to take disciplinary measures. Even failing to accomplish simple tasks properly can earn a maid instructive discipline. It is best for a Mistress to be particular about service so that the sissy maid is not prone to developing bad habits.

Naturally we gave examples of proper punishments. Such disciplinary measures might include putting the sissy into clothing of an infant or to take measures even sterner than that. Common steps may include public humiliation or even the application of corporal punishment. On occasion when poor behavior merits it a Mistress may decide to apply a combination of several methods in order to bring a point home.

Corporal punishment is always applied by the Mistress using a paddle or similar instrument on the bare bottom of the naughty sissy. The intent is to teach her the error of her ways with a much needed dose of humiliation. Humiliation teaches the sissy maid who is actually in charge and the importance of obedience to women. A valuable and useful skill of a good Mistress is to know exactly how to titillate and humiliate her sissy maid with her paddle without doing any actual physical harm.

We also taught that there are other methods of controlling an errant sissy. It is best for a Mistress to use her imagination. Things like a loss of privileges, corner time, early bed times, writing punishment lines, putting the sissy in bondage or holding an uncomfortable stress position are all examples of effective training techniques.

The coeds were always amazed that such methods could successfully be used on a male to evoke suitable behavior. Of course Deanna's presence always served to prove the effectiveness of handling a submissive male in this manner.

CHAPTER 33. Bigger Seminars

The ladies who came to our demonstration generally weren't very sexually dominant. At least when they arrived they weren't. But by the time they left they always had a whole new appreciation for the sexual power of women.

The meetings always began with an introduction and then I would say with a flourish that my boyfriend is my maid before I would summon Deanna with the servant's bell. The humbled maid would then make her appearance with the old-fashioned serving cart. The guests would typically giggle and there would be an occasional gasp when Deanna would present them with a charming little curtsy before beginning to serve them.

Once the ladies had been served Deanna would stand at attention in front of the group with her eyes lowered while I would expound the virtues and amusing delights of having a sissy maid.

When the groups became larger the experience only served to further degrade Deanna. We encouraged the coeds to dress like they were going out on a dinner date so they always looked their best. This served to reinforce their powerful

144

dominance over the sissy maid while giving the ladies added confidence to make use of their sexuality. The maid learned to keep her eyes diverted from the attractive young college students and to keep silent while they enjoyed the seminar.

The coeds would drink wine and bring the maid down a few more pegs with their laughter. It was so amusing to watch because Deanna was helpless to resist them. Her submissive nature didn't allow her to protest her treatment in any way whatsoever.

Carol would then talk about how to handle a submissive sissy maid girl. For these girls Deanna was an object of curiosity as well as an object of ridicule. Regardless of how she was treated she was expected to give them all the respect that they were entitled to as superior women.

While most of the gatherings were informative for the coeds but quite tame sometimes after drinking wine things could get a bit out of hand. At one time or another the girls had Deanna repeatedly curtsy for them and even kiss their feet. On more than one occasion Deanna had to lift her dress and lower her panties to show the girls her sissy clit in order to prove that she was not a real girl but rather that she was just a sissy girl. On another occasion a young coed ordered Deanna to kiss her ass and she shamefully complied.

By far the most memorable session was when one of the girls brought a younger sibling to a meeting. Carol pointed out that even though the girl was just a young teen that submissive males were trained to respect girls of all ages.

At that session a coed asked Carol what would happen if a sissy maid disobeyed an order. It was an innocent enough question and I'm sure that the ladies didn't expect the answer that we gave them.

Carol proceeded to demonstrate to the group how to give a sissy maid a disciplinary spanking. She pointed out the importance of telling the maid what she had done wrong before applying the paddle.

Carol then gave Deanna a stern warning about respecting college coeds before she took the sheepish maid over her lap. The coeds giggled when Carol lifted the maid's dress and lowered her feminine panties.

Carol explained the value of scolding and instructing on proper future behavior while applying the paddle. To the full amusement of the onlookers she then proceeded to spank Deanna while lecturing the maid on the importance of respecting all women.

When she finished applying the paddle she pointed out to the group that Deanna had dribbled precum on her stockings. Carol then explained that sissy girls were often aroused when humiliated, shamed and embarrassed by an authoritative woman. She said that was the key to turning a submissive sissy girl into a sissy maid.

With the demonstration complete Carol then offered the paddle to the other girls to give it a try for themselves. It was embarrassing enough for the maid to have Carol spank her bare bottom in front of such a young group of girls but then the girls insisted that the younger sibling named Wendy who had accompanied them take a turn with the paddle.

The young girl certainly wasn't college age though I have no idea how old that she was. The maid had been serving her wine even though I'm sure that she was under-age for that but it's not like we had asked for identification or anything like that. The maid had even curtsied for the girl several times that evening when serving her because Wendy had told the maid to do so.

When Wendy ordered Deanna over her knees the maid only hesitated for a moment. She took a quick look at Carol with her eyes pleading for mercy that never came. It had to be so degrading for Deanna to humiliate herself like that for such a young girl but she somehow managed to do it.

The other girls shrieked with laughter while Wendy enthusiastically paddled Deanna's bottom like she was a stern baby sitter and the maid had been a naughty child. Wendy grinned with glee while she turned the maid's bottom a deeper red with repeated application of the paddle. All the while she lectured Deanna about proper respect for all girls—even young girls who were new to being a Mistress.

When Wendy finished spanking Deanna she had the maid stand in front of her and thank her for teaching her a lesson. After that Carol produced a disposable diaper and Wendy put Deanna in it while the rest of the girls roared with laughter. Then Wendy triumphantly sent the maid off to stand in a corner facing the wall for the rest of the evening.

We had Deanna keep the diaper on long after the coeds had left. She wasn't allowed to leave the corner or take the diaper off until late that night when we finally dismissed her.

CHAPTER 34. Anita Richardson

While we had extracted our revenge on Deanna
we had no intention of ever letting her leave our
service. After all we had a domestic maid and I
was humiliating her every day at work. But then
unfortunately things went dreadfully wrong.

The company downsized and Carol and I both
lost our jobs. Deanna was let go by the company
too. Then to make matters even worse Carol's
Mom Anita heard about the educational seminars
that we were holding with our sissy maid and
she came by our apartment to find out what we
were doing. Apparently Simone had told her
Mom what was going on in our apartment. Then
Carol's aunt Mildred had shared it with Anita.

I should have known that Anita had ulterior
motives when I saw how she was dressed.
Carol's Mom is quite attractive and when she
arrived wearing a black nylon blouse with a short
leather skirt. Even I could see that those heeled
boots walked into our apartment with a purpose.
She immediately demanded to see Deanna.

Using the servant's bell Carol summoned the
maid from the kitchen. A red faced Deanna
appeared before Anita and gave her a

compulsory curtsy. Anita feigned how appalled she was at such a display of sissy submission. Her eyes flashed at Carol.

"You turned this sweet boy into your sissy maid? What were you thinking?"

Carol had no idea how to respond to that.

"I, we, it was Natalie's idea…"

How thoughtful of Carol to throw me under the bus! I guess that's what friends are for.

"Don't you blame Natalie, I'm sure that you both came up with this idea. I hear that you discipline the maid too. Are you paddling this sweet girl?"

"Why, uh, yes when she deserves it…"

Anita walked over to the maid. On her heels she was taller than Deanna so she looked down a bit on the maid while she gently raised the maid's chin with one finger until they were looking into each other's eyes.

"I dare say that such a sweet girl *does* enjoy her servitude. Yes, submissive sissy girls are like that. But holding seminars at the maid's expense

151

is a bit too much. Perhaps I should take the sissy away from all of this."

The maid was silent. Carol couldn't hold her tongue.

"But Mom…"

"I could use a maid of my own. Come with me."

With that Anita took Deanna by the hand and walked her out of our apartment. The fun was all over.

CHAPTER 35. Employment

A few days later Carol confirmed my suspicion. We had been hoodwinked by Anita Richardson. Deanna was now her personal housemaid and she was doing domestic chores for her just like any hired maid might be doing. Anita was living in the lap of luxury. In the meantime we were unemployed and back to doing our own domestic work in our apartment.

We were both wearing aprons and washing and drying dishes while we talked. I gave Carol a plate to dry while I spoke.

"Carol we trained not one but two sissy maids and yet here we are doing housework!"

"Bad Karma I think."

"It's not fair."

I handed Carol another dish to dry before she continued.

"At least both of our Mothers have live-in maids doing their work for them."

"It's not fair. My Mother has Tillie and your Mother has Deanna. In the meantime we get dishpan hands."

Carol gave a little frown.

"Maybe we should have got the dishwashing machine fixed. Deanna was doing a great job by hand so who would think? Besides who ever said that life is fair?"

We were in serious financial trouble. We were late on our rent and Carol had opened up an eviction notice just that morning. We needed work and we needed it fast. We fretted over our future while we hovered over the sink dutifully doing our dishes.

When we finished washing and drying we sat down on the sofa. That evening Carol was in a panic trolling Craigslist looking for work when the opportunity of a lifetime presented itself.

Help Wanted: House Manager for Weatherford Manor. In need of a domestic to tend to matters of the household. Extensive experience preferred, must be extremely confidential. Also in need of a domestic maid. Room and board plus a stipend for well-qualified applicant. Apply in person.

We were saved! We were ecstatic and we could hardly wait to apply for the job. We decided to go together and get there first thing in the morning so that we would be the first to apply for the positions.

CHAPTER 36. The Weatherford's

We got out of the Uber and stood in stunned silence gazing at the massive mansion. Clearly the owner of Weatherford Manor was a person of means. There a large moving van out in the circular drive and it appeared small next to the house.

We dodged a couple of guys carrying a massive trunk when we approached the front door where a young gentleman stood in his three piece suit observing the workers.

Mr. Tucker Weatherford—we promised to be confidential so don't tell anyone else his name— didn't want us to use his first name. We were instructed to call him "Master" or "Master Weatherford" because we were only the hired help.

He was wealthy to be sure. I had been expecting an older man. I couldn't believe that a young man had accumulated such wealth. I wondered what he could possibly do for a living in order to be so successful. Carol later suggested he must be doing something illegal in order to accumulate wealth like he seemingly possessed. More likely it was probably something in tech but really I have no idea and he made no effort to share his occupation with us.

He eyed us with a certain condescending leer. I was sure that a part of him considered our tank tops and shorts tacky while another part of him seemingly was enjoying the view. He didn't ask us too many questions but I could tell that the first one was the most important.

"Are you experienced domestics?"

Of course we weren't. We had been hotel maids before but we had never worked in a residence. I looked at Carol. She gave a slight shrug of her shoulders before she spoke.

"Why yes of course. I must say that we are very experienced. We only work on a very exclusive basis. Our prior employer was Miss Mabel Cloverlawn in the Hamptons. We've just moved to the area and we are in need of immediate employment. We have heard good things about Weatherford Manor so we are willing to consider service if you are agreeable to accept us."

I had to stifle a hardy laugh. There was no Miss Mabel Cloverlawn and we certainly weren't experienced. Honestly I would need GPS to find the Hamptons wherever that is. I had to credit

157

Carol for her fast thinking. It would work so long as Master Weatherford took her word for it and didn't check our reference. He didn't.

Instead he filled us in on the situation. I learned that the Weatherford's were considering permanently moving south to their winter home but they weren't ready to part with their summer "cottage" just yet. So they had made the decision to keep the mansion for possible future use.

Clearly he was in a hurry to leave the premises. After an extremely short interview process we were both hired on the spot. The job was simple enough. Master Weatherford wanted the mansion occupied in order to keep vandals away. The house manager was to handle financial matters such as paying the grounds keeping company from a small budget. Our job was to keep the place in move-in ready condition in case he changed his mind and returned home.

Taking care of the massive sprawling estate would be no easy task. The two of us would have our hands full just dusting and keeping windows clean. Since Carol didn't like paperwork I was designated the house manager. It really didn't matter though because I would only need to write a handful of checks a month.

The rest of the time I would be a domestic maid too.

To our delight even with the apparently substantial items that Master Weatherford had removed the place remained fully furnished. The amazing indoor pool was a pleasant bonus and I immediately imagined myself lounging poolside with a cool drink.

Master Weatherford told us to report for duty in the morning and that his wife would give us more details. He said not to bother bringing personal effects because everything would be provided for us. That afternoon we arranged for movers to clear out our apartment and put everything in storage with the exception of the clothes on our back.

The next day when we arrived for our first day on the job Mrs. Belinda Weatherford — a young trophy wife if ever there was one — met us at the front door. Much like her husband Mrs. Weatherford was a bit snobby. We were instructed never to use her first name but rather to always call her either "Madam" or "Madam Weatherford". "Her Ladyship" was also acceptable. After all, she pointed out, we were just maids.

Still attempting to play the part of high-class maid Carol managed to divert attention from our attire by asking a question.

"Madam Weatherford may I ask what became of your previous maids?"

"At one time we had four. Marta, Abby and Hilda I think. I don't recall the other girl's name. They didn't take well to discipline and I'm afraid my husband took far too much of an interest in them. I had to let them all go."

With that she showed us to the servant's quarters in the wing at the back of the home. The modest rooms — one for each of us and two more additional identical rooms — were proof that at one time a larger staff had actually tended to the home.

The quarters were hardly more than a bed and a dresser with a small closet. There was one bathroom that was situated near the rooms that was to be shared among the staff along with a tiny apartment sized kitchen for our use.

Her instructions were quite clear and could not possibly be misunderstood. We were to dress in the maid uniforms that were provided in the closets at all times. She didn't want anyone who might see us to think anything but that the house was occupied. She made it quite clear that we were employees — mere servants at that — and that the home did not belong to us. We were to live only in the servant's area and only venture out into the other rooms for housekeeping duties. Sadly my poolside dream was dashed before it even began.

Madam Weatherford then left us to change into our working attire. With a condescending roll of her eyes the haughty Madam told us to change into suitable uniforms and to feel free to dispose of our appalling peasant attire. There was no room she said for such distasteful apparel at Weatherford Manor. She emphasized that garbage day was on Tuesday and that perhaps our clothing should find its way curbside. While she walked away I could hear her muttering something about how Miss Cloverlawn could have possibly put up with such trash. I wondered what she would think if she knew that there really was no Miss Cloverlawn.

That left us to explore our new possessions. Carol went to her room while I opened the dresser drawers in my room. One drawer held rather plain lingerie. The white cotton panties, a cotton bra and a plain slip would not typically be my lingerie of choice. But that was what the job required so I put them on. I tossed my clothes onto the floor and made a mental note to dispose of them later like requested.

The maid uniform was custom made for the Weatherford staff. The simple modest black dress with white trim at the sleeves and collar came with a matching black white trimmed apron and a tiny little lace white cap. Shiny patent leather shoes with three inch heels were the final indignity to the attire of what was certainly a very formal appearing maid outfit.

I have to say that donning a maid uniform was extremely humiliating. The fact that my uniform had *Greta* stitched on the front was a sad reminder that the uniform was clearly second hand and had already been put to housekeeping use. Carol laughed at me when she saw it and teased me by calling me maid Greta. Of course I laughed at her when I saw *Hilda* stitched on hers and I did the same to her.

With that we reported for duty. In a final show of aristocratic snobbery we stood at attention in front of the Weatherford's while Madam Weatherford talked to her husband as though we weren't even present. She told him that she didn't think that we were up to the standards of

Weatherford Manor and that he had to be crazy to entrust the Manor to us.

Once we were suitably chastised before we even had begun to work the Weatherford's were whisked away by a chauffeured limousine off to their new arrogant life.

Carol and I stood in the doorway in our maid uniforms and watched while they were driven down the road and out of sight.

CHAPTER 37. Light Bulb Moment

It had only been two days since the Weatherford's had left us in charge of their estate. After long hours of dusting and vacuuming we still hadn't been in all of the rooms that the mansion had to offer.

The dust never seemed to end. I was sure it was simply moving from room to room while we labored to keep pace. Cleaning Weatherford Manor was a tedious lost cause.

In spite of the workload we had been dazzled by what we had seen. The master bedroom was bigger than the apartment that we had left behind. We took one look at the guest wing and decided to leave all of those rooms for another day. The indoor pool was nestled in a magnificent glass atrium. The pool was so big that it seemed like it could have doubled as a small lake. We dubbed it Lake Weatherford. The dining room could seat a full orchestra while the library could have been a public treasure.

All of that space required constant upkeep just to keep it presentable. We were both exhausted from the effort and we were seemingly losing ground.

At the end of another tedious day we found ourselves back in the servant's quarters cleaning up in the tiny kitchen after a modest dinner. Since the dishwasher in the servant's kitchen was broken we were washing dishes in the sink. Carol was washing and I was drying.

"Carol you realize that in spite of these lavish surroundings we are essentially just fancy maids."

"Oh, you think we're fancy? Madam Weatherford certainly didn't think so."

She gave a little laugh.

"At least we have a place to sleep — even if the little beds are rather lumpy. Is this place wearing off on you? Are you becoming too high and mighty for housekeeping work?"

"It's not what I had in mind when I went to college. Carol honestly I can't do this anymore."

She handed me a wet dish. I carefully dried it.

"What do you mean?"

"I mean the drudgery of housework is too much for me."

She handed me another wet plate.

"The Weatherford's have only been gone a couple of days!"

"I know but it seems like forever. I was thinking."

"Natalie you're in trouble already. You shouldn't think. It takes too much brain power. Just relax and enjoy the free ride."

"I've got a better idea. What if we got a sissy maid to do our work for us? Then we could relax and enjoy our surroundings. The Weatherford's would be no more the wiser and we wouldn't have to wear these silly uniforms any more. That's it *Hilda*. I have to get another sissy maid."

She gave me the last plate to be dried.

"How do you propose to do that? *Greta* you do realize that sissy maids don't grow on trees. It's not like you can just place an order for one."

There were a few moments of silence while I mulled over her last statement. Usually hair-

166

brained schemes are the exclusive domain of Carol. But this time it was my idea to try something ridiculously outlandish.

"Who says that you can't just order a sissy maid?"

"Well it's just not done that way."

"Why not?"

CHAPTER 38. Help Wanted

There are many drawbacks to the Internet. Things can be so impersonal at times. There are so many viruses out there that certainly we are all doomed. But there are also delightful capabilities that only the net can provide. You know, capabilities like those charming help wanted sites. I reasoned that since we had been hired on Craigslist so why couldn't we hire a sissy maid the same way?

That next morning right after breakfast I immediately went to work on my plan. While Carol was busy mopping the immense entrance foyer I went upstairs into Mrs. Weatherford's dressing room to see what I could find to help out.

I needed a little upgrade with my wardrobe to be a convincing employer. A woman in a maid uniform would never be hiring another maid! So I tiptoed into Mrs. Weatherford's closet to see what I could find.

Her walk-in closet was bigger than the all of the servant's quarters combined. I had never seen such a fine collection of gowns, dresses, lingerie and of course shoes. Oh the shoes!

168

The first thing I did was take off my dreaded black heels and slip into a pair of her comfy heels. Until that moment I didn't' even know that Gucci made shoes. I couldn't believe the difference. Clearly her expensive designer designed shoes were better made than the cheap heels I had been cleaning in.

I ventured that if her shoes felt that good then the rest of her clothes would too. So I decided to see how her other clothes felt. I kicked the Gucci's back off and then I took off my cheap cotton panties and bra. I tipped toed over to her lingerie drawers and slipped into the finest black lace satin panties that had ever graced my body.

After that it didn't take any encouragement for me to go all the way. A black lace bra, stockings with a heavenly denier I didn't even know existed and a lavishly appointed half-slip made me feel like a goddess.

I perused her cloths for the finishing touch. A simple striped blouse and a tight black pencil skirt were exactly what I had in mind. I found a cane—the kinky kind used for sensual discipline sessions—hidden behind a few leather outfits at the very back of the closet. I gave a little laugh. Apparently Mr. Weatherford could be a naughty boy but Mrs. Weatherford knew how to handle him.

I sampled a touch of Mrs. Weatherford's cosmetics. I didn't recognize any of the brands that her vanity held. I could certainly never afford any of it but I have to say that imported silky lipstick was simply divine. Her eyeliner, eyeshadow and blush put the stuff that I commonly used to shame.

Once I finished with my makeover I went to find Carol. At first she didn't recognize me when she saw me. For a moment her mouth gaped open when she saw what I was wearing.

"What happened to *Greta*? Natalie you can't do that! We were told…"

"*Hilda* honey, I don't care. I'm taking things into my own hands."

Front that point on it was simple enough. I had Carol take a picture of me holding the whipping cane while I gave my best most authoritative expression. I had one hand on my hip so that I gave the impression that I was not satisfied with what I was seeing. For enticement my striped blouse was left partially unbuttoned revealing a bit of my black bra. I had found a pair of faux black glasses in Madam Weatherford's room that I put on for an added touch of sophistication.

I guess the Weatherford's engaged in all sorts of role-playing games because they seemed to have all of the things needed for it. I could imagine that Mrs. Weatherford must have looked authoritative in those glasses too. Anyway it was the look that I wanted. Carol disagreed.

"You look like an angry school teacher in that outfit. To get the type of help that you want you should display your tempting sexuality not your mean streak."

"Carol it's perfect. Just wait and see."

After that I sat down in one of the offices at the front of the house and used the laptop computer to create a want ad. We both carefully read the bait we had entered on the screen below the picture one more time before I garnered the courage to press enter.

In need of a submissive sissy maid who adores and worships women. Must enjoy housework and be willing to work in uniform for simple room and board. Relationship will be strictly platonic. Sensitive hard working sissy girls only. Tell me why you want to

171

serve me. Respond politely to Madam Weatherford. No brutes may apply.

Carol still wasn't comfortable.

"Are you sure you want to use Madam Weatherford's name?"

"Of course silly. I'll dress like her and I'll garner respect. It will be very believable."

"Natalie I still think that's a bit much. I mean what kind of guy would respond to *that*? All you are going to get are guys who couldn't find your G-spot in bed with a flashlight."

"Precisely Carol. What I'll get is the kind of guy who wants to be my sissy maid. I'm tired of doing housework. I'm tired of guys who don't put me first. Carol we have a good thing going here. While the Weatherford's are away we can play! All we need is a sissy maid to do the work and we will have it all!"

"We'll have all of what?"

"All of what it takes to be happy. I think that my new sissy maid needs to put me above everything else in his life. Oh, and he needs to be able to cook for me, clean for me, do my laundry and know how to properly serve me in bed too!

Others *definitely* need not apply."

I gave a little giggle. I liked the sound of what I had just said. Carol wasn't so sure.

"Serve you in bed? Are you hiring a sissy maid or a gigolo?"

I wasn't about to tell her what I was really thinking. After all a sissy maid can be useful in many different ways.

"Carol you have such a dirty mind. I meant serve breakfast in bed, of course."

"You're asking for too much."

"I don't think so. You just wait and see. Oh and this time we aren't telling our Mothers about what we have going. Deal?"

"Absolutely deal!"

In order to avoid getting Madam Weatherford's clothes soiled I changed back into my maid uniform for the rest of the day. I did keep her

lingerie on and her shoes on too. The temptation
was far too great for me to give them up.

CHAPTER 39. Response

I always enjoy proving Carol wrong. In this
particular case Carol was extremely wrong. By
the time we were finished doing dishes that
evening my in box was stuffed with potential
applicants.

Carol couldn't believe it.

"I guess you were right Natalie. Let's see what
you have."

One by one I opened the responses carefully
scrutinizing each applicant. There were a few
brutes in there that made very naughty sexual
comments even though I had told them not to
bother to apply. Imagine applying for a position
like this and not even being able to follow
directions!

We managed to narrow the field down to five
lucky candidates who seemed to have the girlish
looks that I wanted along with the proper sincere
comments. One youthful looking applicant
named Georgie Corbin stood out from the rest.

"Carol see how he looked down when he took his
selfie? You can tell he was embarrassed to be

applying. Look at that hair. That length could easily be styled into something more appropriate."

"He seems a bit wet behind the ears."

"I like that. We won't have to worry about him needing to unlearn any bad habits. Check out that milky skin. Very nice. Not only that read his comments."

I've thought about sissy maid servitude for a beautiful woman but I've never had the nerve to make my fantasy a reality until now. You take my breath away. You are an angel from heaven Madam Weatherford.

Carol wasn't impressed.

"He sounds pretty sappy to me. Even his name sounds limp. Imagine a boy named Georgie. I think that you found the anti-Clint Steele. What a wimp."

"Precisely what I was looking for."

I quickly keyed in a response.

Georgie I would like to further consider your application. Please sext your credentials along with your height and weight so that I may further peruse your qualifications.

I pressed enter. It didn't take long before there was a reply that included his height, weight and a very obscene photo of his privates. Based on his measurements it turned out that Georgie was girlishly slender. We took a long look at his other credentials carefully scrutinizing his equipment while staring at his tiny qualifications without saying a word. Finally Carol spoke first.

"I was right. He would need more than a flashlight to make much of an impression with *that*."

"In a platonic relationship *that* is exactly what you would want. You do know what *platonic* means don't you?"

"Non-sexual of course."

"That's right. Besides I suspect he is equipped with a tongue and that would be sufficient for my needs I should think."

"His standard equipment is certainly lacking. It's too bad that there's no way to purchase an upgrade. I'm trying to think of other words for tiny. Yes, I would call that a nubbins. Or maybe a sissy clit. Certainly not anything that could possibly satisfy, amuse or interest me."

"I'm doing the hiring here so actually it is none of your concern."

Carol sighed.

"I suppose a tongue would do the job when more suitable equipment is not available."

That's Carol for you. I shook my head.

CHAPTER 40. Coffee House

I had thought it best to meet Georgie in public in a highly visible place. I don't think that a girl can ever be too careful especially after my experience with Clint. We both visited Mrs. Weatherford's dressing room looking for attire suitable for a wealthy employer. We couldn't resist. The designer dresses we selected probably cost a small fortune. They were absolutely perfect. Once we put them on we looked appropriate and we began to feel the part. Then we went over our plan.

I was to be Madam Weatherford and Carol was to be my cousin Madam Harrison. Carol wanted to be Her Ladyship Harrison but I nixed the idea. I thought that would be too obvious that we were not the real thing. We would be wealthy women living together in need of a maid servant. Once we had our story straight we took an Uber to the local coffee shop and we sat there waiting for Georgie to make his appearance.

Before long the slender Georgie with his girlish hair slowly approached our table. He was clearly shy and easily controllable. He was apparently not confident enough to sit down with us because he just stood in front of our table while we looked him over.

He was so timid. The applicant did not disappoint. He waited for me to speak first.

"Hi Georgie. You may address us formally at all times. I'm Madam Weatherford and this is my cousin Madam Harrison."

"I'm so honored to meet you Madam Weatherford."

Carol rolled her eyes. I liked the idea of being on the giving side of snobby. It felt good for a change.

"You may have a seat dear."

He awkwardly sat across from us and immediately began nervously fiddling with his fingers. Carol was disinterested and began paying attention to a stud who was picking up his latte at the counter while I spoke.

"Georgie do you understand what I'm looking for?"

"Yes Madam Weatherford."

He immediately scored points with such a respectful formal response.

"You do understand what a sissy maid is?"

"Yes Madam Weatherford I do."

I smiled. He was so naïve I doubted that he had a clue what I had in store for him.

"To clarify I'm interested in obtaining domestic help in a consensual nonsexual relationship. I'll be taking steps to ensure that our relationship stays that way. While employed you would be required to wear a uniform appropriate for a female domestic worker. Have you thought about that kind of relationship before?"

"Yes Madam Weatherford I have."

"Why aren't you already in such a relationship?"

"I've given it thought but it is a big step for me."

"You don't sound very sincere. You may not be up to the standards of Weatherford Manor. Perhaps becoming my maid isn't for you. Taking you on would require a substantial commitment on my part and I don't want you to waste my valuable time.

181

You do realize that I would expect you to wear a female uniform at all times while you are in service. Most guys have a fetish for maid uniforms and I would think that perhaps you do too or you wouldn't be here. Is that a safe assumption on my part?"

He was so turned on by our discussion he couldn't manage a word. Instead he nodded his head in agreement.

"Most sissies have always secretly wondered what it is like to be a girl. They long for the clothing but they have no idea how a girl really feels. Have you wondered about that too?"

Again he nodded his head.

"Be forewarned. Be careful what you ask for because being a girl isn't all bright sunshine and pretty pink bows. A domestic maid is required to be absorbed in her work at all times. A sissy maid must work twice as hard as a real girl because a sissy maid is only a poor imitation of the real thing. I can be very demanding when it comes to keeping my home clean. Do you understand my terms?"

Carol was quite absorbed with the male getting his latte but she still managed a giggle. I suppose she knew what my own housekeeping standards were when I was the one doing the cleaning back in our apartment. Of course they would be much higher once I had a maid. Georgie nodded his head in agreement.

"If I decide that I like you I would expect a total commitment from you in all respects for a minimum of a probationary three month trial period. During that time I would expect absolute obedience subject to strict disciplinary measures that would be applied at my discretion with no complaints from you whatsoever. I would expect your very best effort and nothing less. Can you do that?"

He paused for a moment to give it thought. The delay was irritating to say the least. Finally he managed to speak.

"Yes…I think I can."

The stud with the latte left the coffee shop and now Carol was paying attention to our conversation.

"You took far too long to respond. Now you must beg me to come to work for me."

I gave him a stern look that I think excited him. That was a good inkling that he was the right subject. He couldn't have sounded more contrite.

"Madam Weatherford may I *please* work for you."

"Work for me like what? I want you to say the words. You know what I want. Say it."

Carol stared at him with a broad grin. She couldn't wait to see if it was possible to humiliate the wimp any further than he already was. She wasn't disappointed.

"Madam Weatherford may I please work for you…as your…sissy maid."

Carol giggled. I smiled.

"That's much better dear. You are to appear at Weatherford Manor next Saturday for your final interview. You are to shave your body as best as you can before I see you again. Only the hair on your head should remain. I'll text you the time and the address."

"Yes Madam Weatherford."

184

I knew that shaving wouldn't take Georgie too long. There was hardly enough testosterone in that little boy to grow any hair at all.

CHAPTER 41. Arrival

We were waiting for Georgie to show for his appointment. I wore the same attire that I had used for the job posting. I wanted to make sure that my intentions were fully understood before I took another sissy maid on. Carol had also fallen prey to the temptation to check out the abundant wealth of high fashion. She was wearing a tiny blue designer dress that flattered her body, showed far too much leg and screamed upscale wealth.

Since the first interview I had been out shopping for my new maid. It had been loads of fun to be seen in public wearing more of Madam Weatherford's clothes. While I was out it had occurred to me that with any luck I wouldn't have to wear that silly maid uniform anymore. When I finished shopping I had stashed a few items in the dresser back in the servants' quarters.

Carol was looking rather puzzled at the only item that I kept at the ready for Georgie's appointment—something I had mail ordered called a Bon4micro cock cage. She made a mystified face at me.

"What is this thing and how does it work?"

"It's a chastity device for—dare we say it—less endowed males. If we are going to have a sissy maid in our house I want to make sure that we are safe."

She twirled one of the six stainless steel scrotal rings that came with the steel cock cage around one of her fingers like it was a tiny hula hoop.

"Where does *this* go?"

"The ring goes behind the scrotum and the cage fastens to it in order to keep a pathetic little cock well-secured. According to the web site it prohibits an erection while any hint of one will cause a certain amount of—shall we say— discomforting pain."

We both giggled at the implication.

"It will remind Georgie to be submissive and it will keep us safe at night. The only way to remove it is with this key."

I held out the gold key that I had placed on a necklace that was around my neck. I planned on keeping the key on me at all times.

"I'm going to need you to install it on him when I give you the signal. When Georgie gets here keep a few cubes of ice handy — you may need it in order to get an initial fit. Stay out of sight until the right time."

"How will I know when it is the right time?"

"Trust me, you'll know."

The doorbell chimes rang. Carol scooped up the Bon4micro and stepped into the office that was adjacent to the entrance foyer. From there she could see the foyer but Georgie standing in the foyer would have his back to her.

I opened the door and there was Georgie. He looked so adorable all dressed up in a business suit like he was applying for an office job. I closed the door behind him and he stood just inside the foyer while I took him in.

Georgie was so bashful he couldn't even look me in the eye. Instead his baby blue eyes were fixed on the floor while I imagined his lovely auburn hair restyled into something much more feminine. Then I thought that maybe I should make him a platinum blonde. Then I decided that I would deal with all of that later.

"Georgie dear I want you to take all of your clothes off so that I can see what you have to offer me. Be quick about it."

In a show of enthusiasm and without saying a word Georgie quickly stripped himself down. He stopped when his hairless body was covered only by a pair of white underpants. When I gave him a blank stare he slowly removed those too.

I could see that his tiny little cock fully appreciated the concept of becoming my sissy maid. It did what it could to show its appreciation in its own little way while I took in the whole picture of a nude job applicant standing in the foyer.

"Georgie I must know the truth about you. Do you truly desire to dress like a female maid and do what is typically referred to as woman's work so that you may experience for yourself what it is actually like to be a woman?"

It was a nuanced question with implications that he most likely didn't grasp but his answer was important. His face turned a shade of red brighter than it had already been.

"Madam Weatherly yes I want to be a sissy maid. For quite some time I've been curious about what it feels like to actually wear lady's lingerie, heels, and other women's clothing while doing domestic work just like a woman might do. I find the thought of it all to be extremely erotic. I've only done so on my own for short periods of time."

"Oh you've experimented with wearing women's clothing before?"

"Oh yes I have. Not too often, just now and then. At first I was just curious but I've found it to be pleasant to say the least."

I heard Carol giggling back from the nearby office.

"Well sweetie if there is one thing you can be certain of it is that I will attempt to satisfy your curiosity. I'm not so sure that you'll find the experience to be pleasant. I hope that you do realize that I'm not interested in a fluffy French maid flittering around in my home like a randy French tart. You must understand that this is a working position.

Sissy girls like you often fantasize about wearing sissy clothing like a French maid uniform. I hope that isn't what you have in mind. Actually the French maid outfit isn't very practical and in fact

190

the attire is really nothing more than a male fetish. I'll have none of that here that's for sure.

Real women don't wear French maid uniforms when they are doing actual housekeeping work. Such attire is reserved for barmaids, strippers or costume parties but certainly not for working women. I don't want a maid who looks like that. I want a sissy maid who can look and act like a real domestic maid. Do you understand what I am saying?"

He nodded in agreement. I suppose that Carol couldn't take the suspense any longer. At just that moment she emerged from the office with chastity device in hand. Georgie gave her a strange look when he heard her approach and then he gasped when she brought him down to size with the quick application of an ice cube to his most intimate appendage.

For him it must have been a blur. In seconds the sissy had the ring secured around his scrotum and the cock cage was in place. From that point on he wouldn't be allowed even a tiny bit of an erection to occur without a substantial penalty. Carol was seemingly quite proud of her accomplishment. She took a few steps back to admire her work and no doubt get her first complete eyeful of the naked sissy.

For the first time the sissy finally offered a hint of assertiveness. He looked down apprehensively at his imprisoned genitalia.

"Madam Weatherford is *that* really necessary?"

"Why of course it is. I did say *platonic* relationship didn't I?"

"Yes Madam but…"

"There is no but. You are either a sissy maid or you are not a sissy maid. There is nothing in between. Now I wonder if you are up to the task. I'm expecting a substantial commitment from you to the job. I can assure you that I intend to not only satisfy your curiosity I intend on showing you what it is like to be an actual maid.

To be honest I don't think any male, even a sissy girl like you, is up to the task of filling the shoes of a real female maid. I actually don't think a sissy girl has the aptitude or the commitment to become a real maid. Tell me, do you really think that you can work in heels all day like a real woman? I'll warn you right now that wearing heels will be a daily uniform requirement and that they will be most uncomfortable for you to work in."

192

Again Carol gave a giggle. We had both been working in those dreadful heels so she knew exactly what I was talking about. I continued to casually lecture the nude sissy who was wearing only the cock cage.

"Most sissies are just fancy crossdressers. They enjoy dressing for a few hours at most for erotic pleasure but that's about it. That's not what we are talking about here. The truth is most are not at all up to the feminine task and the work that it requires.

You have no idea how much time it takes to actually look like a woman. You'll be surprised I'm sure. You'll learn that just putting on makeup and taking off makeup takes a substantial amount of time that you are not accustomed to.

You'll be doing all of that and more. Not to mention the effort it takes to appear well-coiffed. It all takes feminine resolve that you probably aren't familiar with. Sweetie this is your last chance to back out."

I crossed my arms across my chest and gave him an opportunity to reconsider what he was about to do.

"No I don't want to quit. I really want to be your sissy maid Madam Weatherford."

I couldn't help notice his little sissy clit straining against the cock cage. I had phrased being a sissy maid in the worst light possible and yet he was turned on by all of this!

"I see. Well in spite of my reservations about your intentions I will go accept your desire to serve. Remember you are here to clean the mansion and to become the best sissy maid that you can be. This will no longer be your lewd boyish fantasy. It is about to become your actual reality."

CHAPTER 42. Servant's Quarters

I told him to follow me so he obediently walked a few steps behind me while I talked. It seemed odd to be leading a naked sissy through the mansion. I thought about the whipping cane I had found and I wondered if the real Madam Weatherford had ever done the same with her spouse. The thought of leading a naked Master Weatherford back to the servant's quarters brought a smile to my face. In my dreams!

I tried to get my mind back to business. I continued to set the standard for our arrangement while we walked. I wanted Georgie to think that becoming a sissy maid was his idea and that I was doing him a big favor by taking him in.

"Taking a sissy maid on is a huge burden on a woman. It takes a significant amount of effort to teach a sissy maid properly and even if you are satisfactory all I will manage to get out of the deal is a clean mansion. If I make all that effort and you decide to quit then my greatest fear would be realized — that I had wasted my precious time."

"I won't let you down Madam Weatherford."

We reached the servant's quarters at the farthest reaches of the mansion.

"You may find that being a woman isn't the pleasant diversion that you are expecting it to be because I can assure you that it won't be. If you intend to reconsider now is the time. This is your last chance to change your mind."

He peeked into the tiny servant's quarters and then he looked back at me. I gave him a satisfied smile.

"These are the servant's quarters. Once you step into this room there is no going back for you. You will become Abby the maid and you will dress like a female maid and you will be treated just like a hired female servant."

I paused for dramatic effect. Then I took Abby by the hand and led her into her room.

"Abby welcome to your new life. From this moment on you are a domestic maid in the service of Weatherford Manor."

Then I had her lay down on the bed. Carol knew what was next since we had rehearsed our steps well in advance. She opened up a dresser drawer and took out one of the silicon breast forms that I had purchased just for the occasion.

I had actually fretted over the breast forms for quite a bit of time in the store. Sissy girls often have a fetish for breasts so I wanted to make sure that Abby would have plenty of bosom to keep her mind on. After much consideration I had finally decided on a pair of DD forms — they were sure to keep Abby distracted. I also bought the recommended adhesive to go with them. The glue came with an assurance from the salesgirl that it would hold the breast forms in place for a minimum of the three month probationary period that I was offering Abby.

Carol applied the adhesive and then I positioned the forms on Abby's chest. I had her hold still while the adhesive dried. There was a bit of a look of panic on Abby so I thought I would calm her down.

"You said that you wanted to experience what it feels like to be a woman so this is a very important step. While you are in service you will have to wear a bra to support those breasts. You will do so not because you want to wear a bra but because you will *have* to wear a bra. You'll find that those pretty breasts are heavy and they can pull on your skin so you'll have to keep them fully supported at all times. Once the glue is set we'll put you in your bra so that you'll be more comfortable.

A few minutes later with the glue dried we began to get Abby dressed. While I had thought that the lingerie left by the Weatherford's was rather drab Greta seemed thrilled to put it on. In her lingerie she took on the appearance of a young lady getting dressed.

I thought that the poor sissy was going to pass out from excitement when the second hand custom maid dress—already conveniently embroidered with *Abby*—came out of the closet. She slipped it on and zipped it up in back like she was a princess going to a ball. Then she stepped into her three inch heels and tied her apron on.

The look on her face told me that the sissy would be staying at Weatherford for quite a while. If just the attire of a maid had excited her like that I could only guess what putting her to work would do for her.

Abby stood there admiring herself in the wall mirror when the door chimes rang. She gave me an innocent look like she didn't know what to do.

"Answer the door Abby."

"But I'm not ready yet."

I suppose she thought that with no makeup and a hairdo that belonged to a guy she still looked like a guy in a dress and that I certainly didn't expect her to answer the door. She was wrong about that.

"Abby I won't ask you again. I gave you an order and I expect you to hop to it!"

Abby was startled by my assertive tone but nonetheless she replied "Yes Madam Weatherford" and she quickly left the room walking rather awkwardly in her heels towards the front door. Carol and I followed behind her because we knew who the caller was.

CHAPTER 43. Hairdresser

I had called Agnes Tate the day before. We knew her from the apartment complex that we had been evicted from. Agnes was an aspiring actress with a reputation for being a bad girl.

Her mother had sent her off to drama school and she had dropped out after only a few months. More recently she had tried cosmetology school but that didn't last either. When we called she was still living at home and her mother was prodding her to find work.

I'm sure that's why she jumped at the acting job that I offered her. In exchange for room and board with no stipend she was to assume the role of Marta — senior maid at Weatherford Manor. She knew that Carol and I were also acting and that her job would be to transform and supervise our new sissy maid.

When Abby opened the door Agnes was smiling broadly. To the surprise of Abby she went straight past the maid and gave me a big hug.

"It is so good to see you again Madam Weatherford."

"Abby this is Marta our senior maid. She is returning from vacation and she will be training you. She is your supervisor."

I noticed that Marta had brought a few bags with her.

"Marta I see you brought bags. Abby take them to Marta's quarters — last room on the right."

"Yes Madam Weatherford."

With that Abby disappeared down the hallway with bags in hand.

"Marta I told you that everything you need is right here at Weatherford Manor."

"I know but I brought a few wigs, my salon kit for styling hair and my makeup kit. When you said I had to transform a sissy girl I wasn't sure if you had everything that I would need. Abby sure is cute, I don't think it will take much to make her passable."

"Excellent. When she gets back here I'll have her take you to the servants' quarters and you can get started right away. Remember maids at Weatherford Manor are supposed to look professional."

201

"I don't have to do any cleaning right?"

"Of course not. That's our agreement. Transform the sissy girl, teach her how to do her own makeup and hair, train her how to be a good maid and then supervise her. In return you get room and board for as long as you want."

"Best job ever!"

"Get started right away and when you finish both of you report to me for inspection. I want to see how good a job you do."

She gave me a wink.

"Yes Madam."

Abby returned and the two of them went off towards their quarters.

CHAPTER 44. Presentation

While we waited for Marta to do her magic Carol and I made a few decisions. We went upstairs and decided on living arrangements. She would take the largest guest room that also had an expensive stash of luscious feminine clothes and I would take the master bedroom with Madam Weatherford's attached dressing room. That way we would both have separate rooms with our own separate wardrobes.

In the process of finding Carol a bedroom we had stumbled across a room at the end of the corridor. Initially we thought it was a linen closet but when we opened the door we were surprised at what we found.

The room had no windows with only a few simple contents. It contained a wooden chair and a strange looking black padded bench contraption that had straps attached to it. On the wall there were four things hanging on little golden hooks — a whipping cane, a black leather paddle, a tawse and a black riding crop. I looked at Carol for answers.

"What's going on in here?"

Carol walked over to the bench to get a better look. Then she knelt down on part of it and then bent over to lay down over the rest of it. She looked funny in that position with her rear sticking up.

"Natalie you're so naïve. This is a spanking bench. See those implements on the wall? Notice that the whipping cane is identical to the one you found in Belinda's dressing room. It would appear that Madam Belinda likes to play kinky sex games with submissive little Tucker. I don't think that our snooty aristocrats are not nearly as prim and proper as they appear to be."

She gave a laugh and stood up from the bench.

"You mean you think that she *disciplines* him in here?"

"What else could a room like this possibly be used for? It's isolated so the staff wouldn't know what was going on. It's the perfect little getaway for S & M play. Little Tucker could scream his head off while Belinda flailed away on his rear end and nobody would be the wiser."

We chuckled at the thought of the activity that took place in there. Then we went back downstairs to wait for Marta to finish with Abby.

204

Hours went by before the two maids appeared for inspection. In the meantime Carol had found a bikini up in her bedroom and she had gone to the pool for a swim. When Marta brought Abby in I was certainly not disappointed with the work that she had accomplished.

Abby had an entirely different appearance. It started with her hair — a simple short Bob Hair Style with bangs that any schoolgirl could easily take care of. With her maid cap on it gave her an extremely feminine appearance. The look was topped off with a full application of cosmetics that highlighted her blushing cheeks and her pink lips. Her mascara was perfectly applied and it brought out her long lashes.

I was fully in awe of what Marta had done with the sissy girl. She looked like a prim and proper maid certainly most suitable for her position at Weatherford Manor. I gave Marta a big smile.

"Marta you are amazing! Abby looks adorable! I would never have thought you could do such a professional job. She's all yours — be sure to put her to work right away. The tile in the entrance foyer and the tile in the grand hall needs attention. Put her to work on her hands and

knees—that would be a good start and it will put
her in her place.

With that Marta and Abby were off. It was time
for us to have fun.

CHAPTER 45. Life of Leisure

My plan was working perfectly. Over the next few weeks while Marta supervised Abby in tedious domestic chores I took advantage of being the faux Madam Weatherford while Carol basked in the delight of being Madam Harrison. We lived a life that few girls ever get to savor.

Abby cooked, cleaned and tended to our every need. We had her pouring our baths and even helping us dress and undress. Marta taught the maid proper habits until the sissy was so polite that she would bow her head and curtsy when entering and leaving my presence. I felt like a queen and I'm sure that Carol felt the same way.

The first crack in my masterplan appeared when Marta asked me for a favor. It was my first indication that our luck was changing for the worse.

I was lounging poolside with Carol in the Atrium. I had Abby raid the wine cellar and I was savoring a fine glass of wine. The Weatherford's sure knew their wine! Marta slowly approached me before dipping a curtsy.

"Madam Weatherford my I ask for a favor?"

"Sure Marta, what can I do for you?"

"It's Abby. I've come to grow quite fond of her."

"I thought I heard you giggling in her room last night."

"I'm so sorry. We do tend to get noisy. It would be much better if…"

"If what?"

"I hesitate to ask."

It was so uncharacteristic of her to be shy so I knew that she must have wanted something special.

"Out with it Marta!"

"It's the key Madam. It would be *so* much more wonderful if I could have the key to Abby's chastity."

I shook my head.

"Why Marta I'm surprised at you. The chastity is for all of our protection and I certainly would not give you the key. How could we sleep at night

208

knowing that Abby could be tempted to relieve her lust at our expense? Absolutely not!"

Marta gave another quick curtsy.

"I'm so sorry Madam I just had to ask."

With that she returned to her duties supervising Abby. Of course I had already known that Marta was making out with Abby but I felt obligated to protect the young girl. The last thing that I needed was a pregnant maid on my hands.

Over the span of just a few glorious months Carol and I enjoyed the blissful life that only Weatherford Manor could provide. Little did we know that the whole delightful affair was about to come crashing down on our heads.

CHAPTER 46. Return

We decided to go into town and spend more of the money that the Weatherford's had left us for upkeep of the mansion. The account they had designated for such matters was flush with seemingly endless cash so we had been enjoying a life with all of the extras included at no cost to us.

I can still see the scene in my head. The moment is vividly frozen in time like it was this morning. Like every day I had raided Madam Weatherford's closet so I was dressed in a lovely little Yves Saint-Laurent number. I was wearing diamond jewelry that I had confiscated from an impressive hoard that was hidden behind her furs in the dressing room. While I was pilfering jewelry I added a mink stole to my ensemble just for fun. Why wouldn't I? I felt so affluent at that moment attired in fine luxury from my nose to my toes including a lavish use of a most expensive perfume. You know, the kind of perfume that I could never hope to afford myself.

Carol was making full use of her guest quarters attire too. She was wearing the very finest that Giorgio Armani had to offer and she was also wrapped up in a luscious fur. We were two high fashion aristocrats about to embark on the shopping trip of a lifetime.

We had called for a limousine and we were at the front door. Abby was down on the floor polishing the tile while Marta stood over her supervising with a wide grin on her face.

It was pouring cold rain so I had an umbrella in my hand. Just when I ordered Marta to open the front door the door opened up right in front of us and there was Master Weatherford and his wife Madam Weatherford. After a moment of shocking surprise they stepped inside the house bringing wet footprints to the tile that had just been so carefully polished by Abby.

It was the very last thing that I expected to happen. Just like that my world came crashing down in a humiliating thud.

Carol and I froze in stunned position while Abby looked up from the floor at the true owners of Weatherford Manor. Marta was speechless and in what was probably the only gesture that could possibly make any sense at that moment she bobbed a perfect curtsy.

Madam Weatherford was obviously extremely angry when she spoke up. She glared straight at me.

"What is the meaning of this? That's my best Yves Saint-Laurent that you are wearing! My perfume! Girl that perfume is over $1,000 an ounce! How dare you! You…you…"

Thankfully she was so angry that she couldn't think of a word to call me in order to fully express herself. Finally all aghast at what she was witnessing she managed to compose herself enough to raise her voice even louder and give a command. She pointed down the hallway towards the servant's quarters.

"Both of you had better get back into uniform right this instant! Then I want all four of you back here at attention and I will deal with you then!"

Her voice was so loud it echoed off the high ceiling of the foyer and then down the hallway and back. Master Weatherford had a silly grin on his face while the four of us made a hasty retreat from the disaster that had just occurred.

When I reached servant's wing in the room that I hadn't visited in months I quickly changed back

212

into the dreaded maid uniform. I was afraid of damaging the Yves Saint-Laurent so I carefully hung the garment up in the closet along with the rest of the outfit. I decided I would have to sneak everything back into Madam Weatherford's dressing room at my first opportunity.

When my heels clicked back down the hallway to the entrance foyer I found Marta, Abby and Hilda already standing at attention waiting for sentence to be passed.

Madam Weatherford was in no hurry to vent her anger on us. We waited at attention for what seemed like hours before she finally appeared. She had changed her clothes into a little black dress that I had worn for dinner two nights previously. I thought it looked much better on me than it did on her but of course I didn't dare mention that.

CHAPTER 47. *Traditional English Maids*

Master Weatherford was nowhere to be found. Madam Weatherford was going to take on the task of seeing to the servants all by herself. We lowered our eyes while she spoke. Clearly none of us had the courage to look her in the eye.

"I see that my instructions have been completely disregarded. I left Greta in charge with Hilda to assist her. Upon my return I see that Marta and Abby have joined in shameful behavior. My bed has been slept in, my clothes have been worn and disheveled and who knows what other debauchery has taken place in my absence.

You may not have realized it until now but I run a strict traditional Victorian style English household. The most important rule of all is that servants will be disciplined for improper behavior. All four of you are to follow me."

I had expected much more of a scolding than that so I felt relieved. Apparently she had cooled down sufficiently to be reasonable. Or so I thought.

We marched behind her up the grand stairway and it wasn't until we proceeded down the hallway towards the room at the end of the hall that it began to occur to me what might be in store for us. When she reached the door she stepped in first and had us assemble in front of her so that her lecture could continue. She ordered Abby to close the door behind us.

"In the Victorian era maids were disciplined by their Mistress in order to correct errant behavior. Corporal punishment was applied by the lady of the house in full view of the other servants so that they would all be forewarned what disobedience would bring them.

I must say that I enjoy applying such discipline. I think that you'll find that the shame and humiliation will be an incentive to behave properly in the future. She glared at Carol. Hilda step forward."

Carol glanced at me and took a couple of tentative steps toward the angry Madam. The three of us gaped in horror while Madam Weatherford carefully positioned Carol bent over on the spanking table before strapping her firmly down with the belts. Then in an obscene motion Madam flipped Carol's maid dress up and yanked her panties down. The maid looked silly with her bare bottom raised up and framed by the straps of the garter straps holding up her stockings. Satisfied with her work Madam went over to the wall and after a bit of consideration she selected the whipping cane from its golden hook. Poor Carol was held firmly in the humiliating position while Madam continued with her lecture.

"Victorian maids were subjected to childish discipline because it is extremely effective. Hilda you were told to confine yourself to your quarters unless you were doing chores. You disobeyed me."

With that the whipping cane whizzed through the air and slashed straight across Carol's behind leaving a nasty looking red welt where it had struck. Clearly Madam was experienced with the cane. Apparently it took a second before the force of the blow registered with Carol but when it did she gasped in pain.

"Then you dared to wear clothing other than the uniform that was provided for you."

Again the cane sizzled through the air and Carol had a second red stripe adjacent to the first. She flinched from the sting but the restraints held her firmly in position.

Three more times the cane hissed at its target. By the time the fifth parallel welt striped Carol's behind like she was a red zebra she was sobbing and begging Madam for forgiveness. Madam glared at Abby.

"Free the girl. Hilda, I want you to stand and hold your dress up. Face me so that the other girls can see your naughty bottom."

Abby quickly unstrapped Carol. Carol's makeup had run from her tears and she was a bit wobbly but she still managed to pose herself the way she had been ordered to do. She stood with her dress up exposing her welts to us. Abby had an eyeful of Carol's naked bottom while Carol continued to sniffle from her ordeal.

In the meantime Madam returned the cane to the hook on the wall before selecting the riding crop. Then she turned back to Carol.

"The key to proper discipline of young maids is to make the experience addictive for them. That way they don't seek employment elsewhere. There is an interesting relationship between pain and pleasure that has an addictive quality. Perhaps you have never experienced it before."

217

With that she used the tip of the riding crop to gently tease Carol's rosebud. The effect must have been intense because in seconds Carol was gasping in what sounded like lusty pleasure. When she leaned her hips forward to meet the crop Madam laughed and then stopped the stimulation.

"I see that you agree. Quite fulfilling isn't it?"

Carol murmured something that I didn't quite catch. She seemed off in another world of pain and ecstasy that left her vulnerable to the whim of the sadist. Madam Weatherford returned the riding crop to the wall and selected the leather paddle. Then she sat down on the wooden chair. Again she spoke to Carol.

"Over my knees Hilda so that I may finish your punishment."

To my amazement Carol willingly lowered herself over the lap of Madam Weatherford. Then with a gleeful smile Madam began to spank Carol on her bare behind. We watched in horror while Carol screamed in pain and kicked her legs while Madam Weatherford vigorously smacked her bottom.

It wasn't until her bottom was so red that the
stripes from the cane were no longer visible that
Madam ceased her assault. Carol was instructed
to stand with her nose in the corner with her
dress held up by both hands fully exposing her
red bottom. Carol obeyed and looked very much
like a chastised schoolgirl standing with her dress
up showing her rosy bottom with her panties
down around her ankles.

With Carol completely humiliated Madam turned
her attention to Marta. Her next word was rather
dispassionate but its meaning was clear.

"Next."

CHAPTER 48. Next

Marta suffered the same fate that Carol had suffered. It wasn't until she too was standing in another corner holding her dress held up that Madam turned her attention to me.

"Next."

When I was fully secured on the spanking bench she spoke again.

"Greta I'm most disappointed in *you*. Since you were my house manager I expected much more from you. Oh my, you have such a pretty bottom. It's a shame that I should have to discipline it."

I heard the sizzle of the whipping cane followed by a burning sensation on my rear. I wanted to scream but I managed to control myself. I didn't want to give her the satisfaction.

"A maid should know her place. You are going to have to learn your proper manners."

There was another hiss of the cane and a sensation that caused my body to flinch.

"Please Madam Weatherford, I've learned my lesson! Please stop."

The cane whooshed again and my bottom was further tenderized by the sting.

"Poor Greta—already apologizing for her naughty behavior. I sincerely doubt that you've learned a thing."

The cane stung its target again. Tears formed and I began to sob like an errant little girl. Madam wasn't nearly finished. There was another whoosh of the cane through the air. This time it struck me even harder than before. I yelped in pain.

"I'll do anything, I beg you, please stop…"

The cane hissed again. I sobbed like a child while Abby undid the belts that held me in place. I had seen the other girls so I knew what to do. Even without instruction I lifted my dress and faced Madam with my welted backside to Abby. Madam approved.

"Very good Greta—you're a fast learner. I hope that in the future your behavior improves considerably."

Madam exchanged her whipping cane for the riding crop. I really wasn't ready for what came next. When she flicked my clitoris with the crop my heart raced while muscles deep inside twitched like never before. Then the burning sensation on my bottom flared and rushed back to my clitoris. She played with me like that for a few minutes to heighten the conflicting signals of pain and pleasure that my body transmitted directly to my confused brain.

I had never felt such a lewd rush before. It was so embarrassing to succumb to such pleasure at the hand of Madam Weatherford but I didn't want her to stop. I had just enough shame left to prevent myself from bringing myself to orgasm with my own fingers carrying out a desperate act of masturbation.

By the time she finished with me I barely had the energy left to remain standing. My mind was a whirlwind of pain and pleasure. It was a feeling that I never wanted to end. It was practically a relief to go across her lap since my legs were shaking so badly that they almost couldn't support me.

I know that the paddle turned my bottom fully red because it felt like it was on fire. I don't know how long she spanked me but I do know that the stinging sensation lingered when she stopped. Then I went into another corner and just like Marta and Hilda I held my dress up in total shame.

Even though my heart pounded in my ears I could hear Madam talking to Abby.

"My sweet Abby I saw you cleaning the foyer tiles. Apparently you are the only maid here worth her apron. I'm promoting you to house manager. You are in charge of these three naughty maids and they will do precisely what you tell them to do. If they stray the least bit out of line you are authorized to return them here for further disciplinary measures. Do you understand?"

Abby replied in an excited cheerful voice.

"Yes Madam Weatherford."

"For now you are to stay here with these girls. Make sure that they keep those noses in the corners and that they keep those dresses held up high. They are not to touch their bottom for any relief. In two hours put them to work on their hands and knees cleaning the foyer tile — the rain dripped onto the floor when we came in."

"Yes Madam Weatherford."

CHAPTER 49. Bedrooms

It took us forever to clean the foyer and hallway tile. Abby stood over us gleefully watching while we toiled away. By then it was late evening so Abby marched us back to the servant's area without so much as a bite to eat.

Abby had us line up outside our rooms before we were dismissed.

"Ladies I noticed that none of you have shaved your pubes. You are to do so before the end of the day tomorrow. After chores are completed I will be inspecting your work and if I find a single hair you will be reported to Madam Weatherford. Does everyone understand?"

At first I refused to give Abby the satisfaction of a response. Carol was silent too but Marta spoke first.

"Yes Miss Abby."

Abby glared at us. I remembered the sting of the whipping cane. Finally Carol and I both broke down and responded in one despondent voice.

"Yes Miss Abby."

"You are all dismissed."

I went into my room and sat down on the bed. That was a *huge* mistake. I jumped back up from the renewed burning sensation on my blistered buttocks. I stood there wondering what I should do when Carol came in holding a small jar.

"I found this ointment in my dresser. I think it will help. I'll do yours if you do mine."

"Agreed."

I positioned myself down on the bed on my stomach. Carol lifted my dress and pulled my panties down.

"Natalie this looks *really* bad."

"It *feels* really bad too."

She slowly dabbed a bit of the ointment on my bottom. The cooling sensation helped a little. When she finished applying the salve I did the same for her.

After Carol returned to her room I put my nightgown on. The maids wore little frilly nylon babydoll nighties that barely went past our

226

waists leaving far too much exposed under ordinary circumstances. The matching panties covered essentials but that night for the first time I realized why the outfit was appropriate.

The length actually was practical. I left the panty off and positioned myself on the bed on my stomach. It was the only way I could get comfortable with my bottom still burning from my spanking.

In spite of that I was unable to sleep that night. Instead I stayed awake worrying about what was going to happen the next morning.

CHAPTER 50. *Before Dawn*

I was up before dawn so I went to the bathroom
to get properly groomed. Shaving pubes is not
nearly as easy as it sounds. It took quite an effort
not to nick anything so I was at it for what
seemed like hours.

When I finally emerged in my uniform I was
completely fixated on my sex and on my bottom.
With the burning sensation still very present I
had decided to work without any panties. So the
coolness between my legs kept me keenly aware
of what I had done to my lovely pubic hairs.

The combination of stinging pain and heightened
pleasure tantalized me all day. I could tell by the
expression on their faces that Carol and Marta
were in similar states of erotic frustration. Abby
didn't help matters. The sissy maid turned stern
house manager kept us busy with household
chores while carefully keeping an eye on
everything we did. I could feel those eyes on me
too and it only served to worry me that much
more.

It was a good thing that I grabbed a bite before
dawn because Abby didn't give us a break. At
the end of the day we served her in the servant's

228

kitchen and endured the indignity of watching her eat while we stood at attention.

Abby told us we had been bad girls so we were to be sent to bed without our dinner. Then the sissy ordered us to change into our little nighties and report for inspection. We had no choice and soon we were all assembled in the hallway in front of the sissy house manager.

We were ordered to drop our panties and lift our nighties for inspection. Abby gleefully watched while we succumbed to her order for fear of what might happen if we didn't. The three of us stood at attention while Abby looked us over. The sissy began with Marta.

"Very nicely done Marta. Please turn around so that I can see your naughty bottom. Very good. Keep your nightie held high dear."

Abby moved in front of Carol.

"Such a pretty pussy my dear Hilda, why would you ever hide it behind brush? Turn for me please. Very good. Oh dear, that must still be stinging."

Finally Abby stood in front of me.

"My, my a fallen angel. I have big plans for you dear Greta. Turn for me. Yes, Madam did quite a number on your bottom. Serves you right. You have something that I want Greta."

He looked straight at the key that dangled between my breasts.

"No, you can't…"

"No problem. Madam will hear of your insolence in the morning."

"Please don't…"

"The key Greta. Right this instant."

I had no choice. I kept my nightie held high with one hand and surrendered the key with the other. He gave me a devilish grin.

"Three beautiful ladies, what shall I do with you?"

His eyes scanned all three of us at a lewd height I would rather not mention. Finally he gave a devilish smile.

"I know. I'll do all three of you. Marta tonight, Hilda tomorrow and I'll save Greta for last.

Marta come with me. Hilda and Greta you are
dismissed."

Abby took Marta by the hand and led her to her
quarters. Carol followed me into my room.

"Carol what are we going to do? I'm not about to
spend the rest of my life giving blow jobs to a
sissy girl."

"Natalie I don't think a blow job is what Abby
has in mind."

"Oh no!"

CHAPTER 51. Escape

"Carol I'm a virgin. We have to get out of here."

"Natalie you don't have to keep reminding me. I know how virtuous that you are. I'm *not* a virgin and I *still* want to get out of here. This has been so humiliating! Do you have any money? If you do we can call for an Uber and be out of here while everyone is sleeping."

"I'm not so sure that Marta is going to get any sleep tonight but yes I do have money. Sort of."

"Great. Sort of? What do you mean by that?"

I didn't want to give her the bad news but I had to.

"It's in my purse. Upstairs underneath Madam Weatherford's bed. Do you have any money?"

"It's in my purse upstairs under my bed."

"We can't risk going up there. If we are caught…"

"I won't be spanked again. It hurts just thinking about it."

232

I had no argument with that. We pondered the situation for a few moments. Finally I made the decision.

"We'll have to just go for it and leave. How far can it possibly be to town?"

"Then what?"

"We'll have to improvise."

"Okay."

We couldn't very well leave dressed in our nighties so we turned ourselves into maid Hilda and maid Greta again. Once we were back in uniform we were ready to leave. I still wasn't wearing panties but I did manage to put a pair in my apron pocket just in case.

Once we were back in the hallway we could hear Marta being bedded by Abby. She certainly wasn't making an effort to resist. Apparently she was putting out for the sissy big time. Her unbridled moans of ecstasy emboldened us to leave. I was certainly not going to give Abby the satisfaction of fucking *my* brains out. As if that was even possible with the tiny equipment the sissy had to work with.

233

We slowly tip-toed down the hallway, through the mansion and out into the cool night air. Even with a half-moon shining it was dark. Carol pointed out the glow of lights on the horizon that indicated civilization. We set off down the road in that direction.

We kept looking back over our shoulders but there was no pursuit. We seemingly walked for hours while the lights grew brighter. Our heels were definitely not made for covering long distances and by the time we reached civilization my feet burned almost as bad as my bottom.

Our escape was exciting. Or maybe it was just my slip swishing against my naked sex while we walked. Whatever the reason by the time we approached a large hotel I was titillated beyond belief and not really thinking straight.

I don't know what I thought we could do in the lobby of a hotel at 3:00 in the morning with no money and no luggage but we gave it a try. Fortunately for us the lady behind the counter was the early morning manager. She smiled at us when we approached.

"Hi I'm Sylvia the hotel manager. What have we here? Another Greta and Hilda? I presume you are both from Weatherford Manor?"

"I looked at Carol. She was surprised just like I was. I took the lead."

"Why yes, how did you know?"

"The uniforms scream Weatherford Manor. I seem to see a new Greta and Hilda every time the Weatherford's return from their vacation down south. I don't know what's going on over there but I've always benefited from those who leave their employment. I suppose you have no money."

She seemed to know our situation well.

"Why…a… no…we don't."

"I can offer you girls the standard deal I give all the Weatherford girls. If you commit to maid service here at the hotel for ninety days I can give you room and board. I also pay a dollar a day each but you won't be paid until the end of your ninety days. After that you can go wherever you want. Take it or leave it."

Under the circumstances it sounded great. I glanced at Carol and she nodded.

"We'll take it."

"Good. I don't have any girls working the fourth floor."

She gave us a card key.

"Room 499 is the maid's room at the end of the corridor. It's all that I have. You can share the twin bed. Start cleaning at 6:00 am. If you're good at it you should be finished by 3:00 pm. If that's too much work for you I'll terminate both of you. You *are* experienced maids right?"

This time Carol chimed in. She knew that I would tell the truth and it wouldn't get us what we wanted.

"We're Weatherford maids Ma'am. Of course we are experienced!"

"Very well. Off with you both. There are clean uniforms in the closet in 499. Clean yourselves up before you start. You both look like the cat dragged you in. I'll have none of that in my hotel. Dinner is at 5:30 pm in the employee

236

lounge on the first floor so don't be late. Have a nice evening Greta and Hilda."

We responded in chorus.

"Yes Ma'am."

That was how we escaped Weatherford Manor and managed to become employed just like real maids.

CHAPTER 52. Sleep

We fell asleep right next to each other on the twin bed. We were so exhausted that we didn't take the time to undress. We must have looked silly in our uniforms on our stomachs with our dresses hiked up exposing our red bottoms but it was the only way that we could get comfortable.

It was 6:30 before we woke up that next morning. Sylvia was right. There were fresh uniforms in the closet—two each embroidered Hilda and Greta. It seemed like a cruel joke but I'm not kidding about that. We decided not to fight it any longer. While we worked at the hotel Carol would remain Hilda and I would remain Greta.

Even better the tiny dresser held cotton panties and cotton bras. I had the distinct feeling that many Weatherford maids had come through the room and that they had all been in a situation similar to the one that we were in.

We took turns showering. The warm water felt like acid on my bottom but felt titillating on my shaved pubes. I decided it was still best to go without panties at least for one more day.

Fortunately Sylvia didn't check on us. So when we began cleaning rooms at 7:30 am we had a late start but nobody noticed. We spent the rest of the day trying to catch up so that we would finish the last room on time.

I suppose that experienced maids might have finished on time. Sadly in spite of Carol's boast we were certainly not experienced. It was 8:00 pm when we staggered into the employee lounge exhausted from the effort we had put out.

Sylvia was nice enough to have left each of us a plate filled with much needed nourishment. There was a note on top of mine.

Nice try ladies. Experienced maids my ass. Better luck tomorrow.

— Sylvia

I grinned at Carol.

"I guess she saw right through us."

"But she hired us anyway."

"Oh great! A pity employment. It's come to this!"

We reheated the food in the microwave. Leftovers never tasted so good.

I suppose it served us right. Over the next ninety days Carol and I were proper hotel maids completely engrossed in changing linens, cleaning toilets, vacuuming floors and emptying waste baskets. Working in a hotel in a maid uniform is a daunting task that gives one an appreciation for other possible career paths. Guests always expect the best from you while treating you like a lowly servant. We did collect a few tips but they were few and far in between.

We both learned that being a maid is no easy task. We also learned a bit of respect for the work that sissy maids do. Of course it only served to emphasize our own desire to have a sissy maid of our very own. After working for ninety days on the fourth floor I vowed that I would never do another housekeeping chore ever. At least if I could help it.

CHAPTER 53. Reanna Deardon

You might think that being a hotel maid is a boring job. While the actual work is pure drudgery it was the occasional surprise that broke up the daily mundane chores and kept us from going insane.

It was not unusual to find panties, a bra or even condoms that had been left behind by guests. Carol and I would laugh at the variety of enticing things that no doubt were misplaced after a night of intense passionate lovemaking.

By far the most interesting week that we had occurred during the software convention that was held at the hotel. That week every room was booked so there was plenty of work for us to do. Our surprise came on Monday morning when we opened the door to room 421 and found Miss Reanna Deardon waiting for us.

While typically guests would have a do not disturb sign on the door when they were in the room Miss Deardon did not do that. Her intention was specifically to talk with us.

When we entered 421 there she was sitting at the vanity table carefully applying her lipstick. She was rather young for the convention crowd but she was dressed to fit right in by wearing a prim and proper navy blue pinstriped skirt suit. She appeared very no-nonsense and extremely professional. Even her auburn hair was perfectly styled and put up much like any authoritative business woman might decide to wear it.

So you can imagine our response when unlike most guests who simply ignored us Miss Deardon immediately engaged us in conversation.

"Ladies I'm so glad to see you. I have a proposition for you."

We both stood in front of her curious what a woman like her could possibly want from a couple of hotel maids like us.

"Are either of you familiar with submissive males?"

I looked at Carol and we both giggled at the same time. Miss Deardon had definitely come to the right hotel maids with that question. We nodded our heads.

"Very good. Let me further explain. Two years ago I came to this very same convention with my boss Denton. We had adjoining rooms that year — in fact this very room. One evening I went into his room to see if he wanted to go out to dinner together and I found him in a rather uncompromising position."

Carol smiled.

"We get that quite a lot here."

"Not like this. I accidently found out that Denton was a crossdresser. When I went into his room he was in full lingerie and he was making himself up for a night out on the town. He was even wearing a ladies wig that flowed down to his shoulders!

Well you could imagine my shock when I saw him like that. But when I saw how embarrassed he was I decided to take advantage of the situation."

I had no idea where she was going with her story but it was certainly riveting.

"Denton wanted to change his clothes but I insisted that he attend the convention dressed up like a woman. We spent that evening together talking about his desire to wear female clothing. After that I referred to Denton as Debbie.

243

Since that eventful evening I took charge of Debbie and became the boss at our company. Debbie has become my secretary. So we are attending the conference again this year with Debbie as my office secretary."

I gave a little giggle but I was still a bit confused.

"Miss Deardon may I ask what that has to do with us?"

"Perhaps it would be best if I show you."

CHAPTER 54. Denton

Reanna walked over to the door that separated the adjoining rooms. She opened it up and motioned for us to follow her into the adjacent suite. We had just passed by that room because the do not disturb sign was out.

Like I said hotel maids see the strangest things but nothing prepared us for what we saw that morning. Reanna pointed to the king sized bed and smiled.

"That's Debbie."

Debbie was dressed only in a black bra that was well padded out, a black garter belt with stockings and black panties that were clearly bulging out in a most lewd and obscene manner.

Debbie was tied spread-eagled on the bed with silk scarves. Though she was effectively silenced with panties that were stuffed in her mouth and secured there with a silk scarf I could see that she was well made up to look just like a woman.

I was shocked to say the least. Carol's mouth gaped open but no words came out. We both looked at Reanna for an explanation.

"Ladies I've decided to add to Debbie's duties."

When Debbie realized that there were women in the room other than Reanna she started to pull at the scarves that held her in place. She was well restrained though so she was only able to helplessly wiggle and squirm. Reanna continued.

"I want Debbie to become my housemaid. But she is woefully inexperienced in such duty. I was hoping that the two of you might take her under your wing this week and train her."

Once Debbie heard that she began to shake her head no. She attempted to verbally protest but all we could hear were muffled sounds coming from beneath her panty sandwich. Reanna ignored the obvious protests.

"She is really quite docile and willing to accommodate whatever instruction you might decide to give her. Let me demonstrate."

Reanna sat on the bed next to Debbie. She pulled the front of Debbie's panties down and the erect penis sprung out in a lewd display of taut arousal. Reanna tenderly took hold of the swollen member with one hand and with one finger from the other she began to gently circle

246

the glans in a teasing motion that brought an immediate response.

We could hear blissful moaning coming from Debbie from beneath the gag. Reanna continued in a soothing voice while she tantalized the sissy.

"Debbie I've brought maid Greta and maid Hilda here to teach you how to be a proper maid. These are very pretty ladies and I must say that they will be firm and strict with you. I want you to nod if you would like to work with them this week as their junior maid."

Debbie quickly nodded her head in total agreement.

"There there, that wasn't so bad now was it?"

Debbie made a contented cooing noise while Reanna continued to stroke the tip of the firm erection.

"Excellent."

Reanna stopped her teasing and turned back to us. Debbie made a sound like she was begging for more.

"Ladies if you come back after you clean my room I'll have Debbie dressed and ready to go."

I looked at Carol. She shrugged her shoulders and we went back into Reanna's room to clean.

When we returned a short time later Debbie was dressed in a maid uniform that was identical to the uniform that we were wearing. Obviously Reanna had planned ahead and was well prepared for what she had done.

There was no visible evidence that the maid was anything other than female. In fact her slim build, perfect makeup and sharp uniform made her indiscernible from any of the maids who were also hard at work in the hotel. She would easily be able to participate in maid duties with us without drawing attention.

Reanna went on to attend the conference while we trained Debbie. She turned out to be just as submissive as promised. For a full week Debbie never once complained about her duties. Instead she obeyed us like we were her superiors. Of course we actually were.

Debbie turned out to be exactly what we needed to cheer us up. She worked with us every day doing housekeeping duties just like any other

248

junior maid might. Naturally we gave her all of the dirty jobs that we didn't really want to do. I don't know how many toilets that Debbie cleaned that week but I can say that she did them all.

When it was time for Reanna and Debbie to leave it was like our vacation had ended. Reanna thanked us for training Debbie and asked if she had been sufficiently obedient for us. Reanna offered to have us apply the paddle to her sissy girl but we said that was not necessary.

After that the two of us were back to doing all of the work ourselves.

CHAPTER 55. Visitor

On our final day on the job we had a surprise
visitor. When we went to check on room 400—
the presidential suite—we found Madam
Weatherford patiently waiting for us. She was
sitting like a queen looking fantastic in a chiffon
dress by Christian Louboutin. I recognized it
because I had worn it myself. A couple of times
actually.

I remembered how delightful it flowed over my
body. I'm sure if Madam would have realized
that I had taken the dress for a spin or two she
wouldn't be wearing it but I guess I had done a
good job of having the dress cleaned.

Anyway it took me a double take to realize that
the juvenile appearing girl standing next to her
was Abby. The sissy was dressed like a young
school girl complete with blouse and jumper
identical to what the girls in the local private
elementary school were required to wear. Her
hair was in pigtails adorned with tiny little pink
bows. Her makeup was overdone in pink
including glossy pink lipstick. Her nails clearly
had extensions and were done in glossy pink that
matched her lipstick. Her humiliation was

capped off with shiny pink classic Mary Jane shoes.

When I realized the schoolgirl was actually Abby I gave a little giggle. Carol did the same. Madam smiled at me.

"I see that you approve of my junior maid. I can assure you that she has had quite the come down since I found her attempting to mount Miss Marta. Such behavior is not acceptable at Weatherford Manor! Weatherford Manor has never before witnesses such scandal. I can assure you that Abby has been suitably disciplined and that it will never happen again."

She fingered the gold key that was dangling on a necklace between her breasts. Abby stayed silent with her eyes lowered. No doubt she had felt the sting of Madam's whipping cane and knew better than to say a word.

"Now that you've been properly trained in maid service I wanted to come and offer you both a position back at Weatherford Manor. I understand now what happened and I commend you both for how you handled this incompetent sissy girl. Greta of course you would be in charge of the girl and you could discipline her at will. Good help is so difficult to find so I would like you both back at twice your previous rate. I'm sure you'd agree that is quite an offer."

Actually it was!

I wanted time to consider her offer so I thought I would try and engage her in conversation.

"Madam I meant no disrespect. I thought that you were moving out. I mean I saw the moving van, right?"

She gave a little laugh.

"Oh that. Actually they were bringing in new furniture and removing the old stuff. We like everything fresh when we come back from vacation."

"But Master Weatherford said…"

"He likes to do that to new employees. It's a test. You failed, of course."

I thought I should quickly change the subject.

"Madam, may I ask, how did you find us?"

"We own the hotel of course. I can assure you that it is one of our many holdings. Sylvia is my sister-in-law and she keeps me posted. She tells me that you've both become quite accomplished at housekeeping since you arrived."

I have to say that I was actually considering her generous offer. I guess for just a moment I forgot how employees at Weatherford Manor are treated for improper behavior. When Carol spoke up I realized why Abby was standing rather than sitting and I came to my senses.

"Thank you Madam for your kind offer but we really can't accept your most generous offer. Today is our last day working here and then we will be on our way."

Madam was clearly disappointed. I suppose she isn't turned down very often when she offers big money.

"Very well Greta and Hilda. I wish you both the best."

She pointed to the large king-sized bed and the two purses that were on it.

"I had Abby carry over your purses. Marta found them in the Mansion and I thought that they should be returned. You'll both find full

253

payment for your services at Weatherford's inside."

With that she gracefully rose out of the chair and motioned to the sissy girl.

"Come with me girl. We are off for some shopping. After that I'll be taking you to the salon with me to have your hair colored."

Madam spoke to me while she passed us by.

"She would make a fetching blonde don't you think?"

With that we saw the last of Madam Weatherford. We could only imagine how firmly Madam treated her junior maid. She would not be lenient with her — that was for sure.

In my mind I envisioned Abby in her uniform bent over the spanking bench with her dress up and her panties down. It would have been worth working just a few more days at Weatherford Manor just to see her get what she had coming to her.

CHAPTER 56. Homecoming

When Sylvia cashed us out after our ninety days we thanked her profusely for the opportunity that she gave us. Then we left dressed the same way that we came — in our Weatherford Manor maid uniforms. It was the only attire that we had.

We set off from the hotel in separate Ubers. Carol went back home to her mother while I went back home to mine. We were broke and unemployed. We both felt that under the circumstances it was best to throw ourselves at the mercy of our mothers. Since they both had sissy maids at least then maybe we wouldn't have to do any more housekeeping chores.

Mother was happy to see me. She threw her arms around me and gave me a big hug. We chatted for a while before I realized that Tillie was nowhere to be seen.

"Mom what happened to Tillie?"

"Oh she tired of all the housekeeping work and decided to move on. I guess being a sissy maid just wasn't for her. It was poor timing. I had just shown her off at another tea party to all of my friends and everybody had thought that she was so cute.

I think it's Anita's fault. She taught her far too much French. Tillie said something about a burlesque cabaret in Paris or some such utter nonsense and then she went right out the door French maid uniform and all. Imagine that!

I see by your uniform that you envied the maid. It looks custom. Do I sense a new career? You could do worse. A new look? It suits you. A new name? Well maid *Greta* dear you've come to the right place because I need a new maid."

"It's not like that Mom…"

"I'm sure maid Greta. The good news is that I have plenty of work for you to do. Nothing has been done since Tillie left. Plus she left her uniforms so all you have to do is change the embroidery to read *Greta* and you are ready to go. I wouldn't want to call you Tillie now would I?"

"No Mom…"

"It's agreed then. You can be my maid. I've had to go without a domestic since Tillie left and it has been a burden. Maids don't grow on trees

256

you know. It's not like you can just place an ad on Craigslist and get a good one. That would be silly to even try. You know what kind of a response you would get with that."

"But Mom…"

"Don't worry Greta dear. You may have failed at your previous domestic job but I'm sure that I can train you up to standard. You can start with the laundry. It has been sitting there for weeks. Hop to it maid Greta, you wouldn't want to disappoint your new Mistress!"

"But Mom…"

"Greta I see the logic in your career choice. It will make good training for being a future housewife. A woman's work is never done! I am surprised though, you've never shown much interest until just now. Off with you sweetie!"

She pointed towards the laundry room. I couldn't believe what was happening. I could see that there was no point in arguing with Mother so I went to the laundry room to get started.

I couldn't believe the mountain of clothes I found piled up on the floor there. Since I already had an apron on I went right to work.

257

I was hand washing lingerie when I thought I would check up on Carol. She had to be doing better than I was so I thought she might cheer me up. I put her on the speaker on my cell and we talked while I worked.

"Carol you won't believe what I'm doing. Tillie has left for Paris and Mom has a pile of laundry that will take me all day to finish. So I'm still in my maid uniform and I'm doing chores. She wants me to be her housemaid! Can you believe it? How are you doing? Give me good news!"

There was a pause on the other end of the line.

"Natalie I'm still in uniform, Mom is calling me Hilda and I'm doing laundry too! Mom said that Deanna left a few days ago. She said Deanna said something about not wanting to be a maid anymore. Mom is putting me to work as her maid! I'm back home but I feel just like Hilda."

"Well that makes two of us. I feel just like Greta."

We both laughed together. I smiled while I patted dry a pair of Mom's panties. I wasn't ready to give up just yet.

258

"I think what we really need is our very own sissy maids."

"Agreed. But you know they don't grow on trees. Don't even think about Craigslist!"

"I made one mistake and I suppose that you'll never let me forget."

"Natalie I promise! I won't ever let you forget!"

Then Carol sounded serious.

"Natalie do you think that we are being punished by our Mothers?"

"Of course we are. They weren't very happy that we went out on our own."

Carol sounded wishful.

"I hope that our punishment doesn't last very long."

"It won't."

"Why not?"

"My brother Stevie is coming home from college. If we can find work we can get our own apartment…"

Carol got the idea real quick and finished my sentence.

"…and I can talk him into being our maid!"

Carol was right about that. There's nothing that brings a boy to heel like putting him in panties, a well-padded bra and a maid uniform.

It had been a crazy time for us trying to find the perfect spouse. We both vowed to continue our search for our very own submissive sissy maid.

In the meantime we are both still single and we are both still searching. Though we are both still doing housework we are waiting for Stevie to come home from college so that we can put him to work. Until then we are both still working for our Mothers.

ABOUT THE AUTHOR

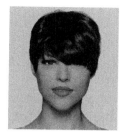

Miss Natalie Deshay grew up on the West Coast next door to her neighbor and best friend Carol Richardson. They both attended the same schools and while they were in school they both spent several summers working at a national lingerie shop.

Today Natalie is a substitute high school teacher. Her hobbies include tennis and racket ball. She also likes to read and write in her spare time.

Carol became a nurse and she now works in a medical clinic near her home. She is also an amateur photographer and illustrator.

They remain the very best of friends and still live on the coast sharing an apartment together.

The enticing books of Natalie Deshay are the shared sexual fantasies of Natalie and Carol. Their stories celebrate the enduring superiority of strong women and those who serve them— particularly feminized sissy males.

Just like Natalie likes to say, "My suitor needs to rock my world and put me above everything else in his life. Oh, and he needs to be able to cook for me, clean for me, do my laundry and know how to properly serve me in bed too! Others need not apply."

Both Natalie and Carol are still waiting for the male of their dreams to succumb to them and bring their erotic fantasies to life.

The provocative works of imaginative fiction by Natalie Deshay touch on the fantasies of women everywhere who relish dominating and sissifying males for the fun of it.

You'll enjoy all of these sensual works from Miss Natalie Deshay.

Tempting Foundations

Natalie explores her dominant relationship with her younger sissy brother Stevie when he finds himself employed in a ladies lingerie shop.

263

A young panty thief is taught that there can be severe consequences for getting into ladies panties without an invitation.

Sissy Maid School Teacher
Natalie and Carol discover that their hot male teacher wears women's panties! Naturally there is only one thing they can do with *that* information. Soon Natalie and Carol are the teachers and their former teacher is kept busy with learning a lesson in domestic servitude.

Sissy Identity Crisis
You won't believe what happens to her sissy brother when a strict disciplinarian, a sexy English teacher and a dedicated school nurse all come together to lovingly help the sissy out. In this timely gender bending fantasy Natalie explores the ramifications of a school transgender bathroom policy gone unexpectedly awry.

My Sissy Brother
Mystery revealed! For the first time Natalie Deshay shares the intimate story of how her close friend Carol Richardson discovered sissy girls. When it comes to sissy girls most women aren't cruel or heartless. We tend to be understanding and compassionate. Of course helping to tutor a sissy in proper behavior can be a big responsibility for a big sister!

wardrobe Miss Ellington decides to take action.
What do you do with an ill-mannered nephew
who likes to wear your clothes? If you're
Millicent Ellington you summon Natalie Deshay
so that she can practice her special set of tutoring
skills on the naughty youth. Will Patrick be
brought to heel? Will he end up in heels? Find
out for yourself in this titillating sissy maid
adventure!

Skeffington Academy For Girls

Even dominant women are capable of enjoying
the forbidden thrills that sexual submission can
bring. Sissy girls aren't the only girls who are
able to enjoy the thrill of breaking tradition. In
Skeffington Academy For Girls the reader
explores the taboo world of sexual submission.

The reader is carefully led into the secret society
of the Skeffington Academy For Girls and learns
about the forbidden pleasures of submission.
Follow the fantasy of Miss Natalie Deshay into a
world of secret pleasures while she uncovers the
truth about Skeffington Academy. If you dare to
enter you'll soon find out that nothing at the
Academy is what it seems to be.

The Naive Dominatrix

Natalie recalls how innocent she was before she
began to work with sissy girls. There can be

regrets in life and Natalie shares how she may have done a few things differently along the way if she had a second chance.

A new employee upsets the culture at the all-female Blushing Cosmetic Queen company. Natalie and Carol know precisely what to do with an employee who just doesn't seem to fit in.

Printed in Great Britain
by Amazon